Major Pain

Courtney Brandt

CONTENTS

Chapter 1: The Decision

I'm not sure why, how or when I came to this decision. In my prior three years of marching band, I hadn't been a section leader and I had no previous leadership experience to speak of, but something compelled me to, and the feeling wasn't letting up. I'm sure my twin brother, Jude, would tell me my new out of left field life goal was because of my recent decision to break up with my boyfriend of forever, Everett Wallace, but I'm telling you differently.

I, Rigby Sullivan, was going to audition for drum major of the Parktown Pirate marching band.

I know, big deal, right? In the whole history of the world, there were a lot more significant choices. However, for me, in my own little life, this decision was as big a change as I could make. First of all, for as long as I could remember, no one from the drumline had ever attempted this transition. Drum majors for our sad little excuse for a marching band had always come from another section – usually a brass player, but sometimes an ambitious saxophone or flute would slip in and rise to the highest leadership role in the band. Percussionists stayed in the Line, with center snare and percussion captain being the highest placement possible. Furthermore, if there had ever been a drumline member in the history of the band who had been awarded drum major, they certainly hadn't been some semi-talented third bass drummer.

So far, I hadn't told anyone about my decision. Not Jude or any of my friends. Definitely not Everett. I knew that no one in the Line would understand. They would make fun of me and tell me I was already in the best section. Maybe they were correct, but something about my upcoming senior season wasn't going to feel right if I was playing bass for a third year (tenors were out of my realm of possibility, and the snare line was a bit too close to my ex-boyfriend for comfort). Plus, there was a rumor we were getting a new drumline instructor, and the thought of starting all over again with some college kid trying to prove himself with us was something that didn't interest me in the slightest. More than anything, deep down I knew there wasn't going to be room in the drumline section for me with Everett as captain. We had too much history. Up until the recent breakup, we had been known affectionately as 'Mommy' and 'Daddy' to the section – keeping the peace, breaking up arguments, and making sure everyone was included. As Everett and I had planned it, our senior year had all sorts of possibilities. We had grown up together, started as naïve freshman, dated since forever and had long conversations about how our final season would go – the pranks, the cadences, the practices – all that seemed in the distant past now.

Had my decision to audition for drum major had an impact on me deciding to break up with Everett? Maybe. But then again, maybe I wanted something different. I didn't have anyone else I was interested in, just the yearning to want to make our band better. It was as if some switch had gone off in my head one morning and now that it had been activated, there was no going back.

Jude, of course, intelligent as he is (he is first in our class, after all), would probably tell me the desire to lead the band was an unconscious need to one up my ex-boyfriend. My twin had an annoying habit of being right all the time – most obnoxious. Yes, being drum major was the ultimate position in the band, and the only one who could tell the drumline captain what to do. However, as far I knew, while Everett and I didn't have any issues about who was 'the boss' in our former relationship, I could understand what Jude would hypothetically tell me. So what? I didn't think there was anything wrong with stating my independence with an obvious gesture.

Perhaps I should explain we had been the perfect marching band couple – royalty among the band geeks at our school. We had started dating our freshman year at band camp, and the recent breakup had shocked everyone. If I was totally honest with myself, I knew I ended things because the prospect of being drum major had become more interesting than dating him. Everett was more a friend than someone I had romantic feelings for, and I wasn't doing either of us a favor by staying together. I had come to my realization over the past couple of months, but had only recently had the strength to actually follow through with ending things between us. I had gritted my teeth and smiled through Prom pictures, knowing it would be too mean to call things off. I had lasted four days after the big event before I tried to let him down as gently as possible. I still cringed when I thought of the awkward conversation. He hadn't believed me at first – wouldn't accept what I was doing. Since then, we'd taken to avoiding each other and I hoped this pattern of behavior would not last into the season in the fall.

So, without Everett to concentrate on or take up my time, all I could do was think about were the upcoming auditions. As I far as I knew, there was only one drum major spot open. The marching Pirates (yargh!) were roughly 75 strong and had a leadership team of two. And to clarify, we're nothing special. In fact, we're the band that is the joke of the entire district. I have no idea why our band director, Ms. Jenkins, has us compete in anything, because we always get the lowest score. In my three seasons, our highest placement was maybe 8 out of 10 competitive bands, and when that happened, we totally celebrated. We're not the band that wins awards. We barely show up to practice. There wasn't any particular reason for why we sucked year after year, but I had a feeling that if we wanted to, we could be a much better band. We had the talent, a lot of supportive band parents, and even Ms. Jenkins was halfway enthusiastic. We just needed some other dynamic that wasn't currently being met.

On some level, I guess, maybe, rather than my legacy being one half of Rigby and Everett, maybe I felt a weird need to make our marching band something worth remembering. Don't get me wrong, being in the Line was a blast, but there were only so many times you could watch the same marching programs win, year after year. I know we all tried to play it off like we didn't care, but when you're a drummer, there's a weird cocky thing that goes with the territory, and being dumped on by every other Line you know is not particularly a fun position to be in. The discipline we didn't have was reflected in the rest of the band. We would learn the show, and the halftime performance would be okay, but we never seemed to get around to perfecting all the parts. The diagonals never locked, people were always out of step, and there were times when phasing was so bad, you couldn't even tell what we were playing. Although no one would admit it, the whole thing was all pretty embarrassing. Sure, we didn't have to work hard and practice was merely an excuse to get together and go through the show a few times, but given the chance, I thought we hadn't come close to reaching our potential.

I wanted this year to be different. We could make a difference to the underclassmen and the 8th graders who were going to join the band. I had heard a lot of good things about the class coming up, and was hopeful their influence could mean something.

Once I realized my goal of becoming drum major wasn't going anywhere, in preparation, I had been practicing every day after school. If I was going to commit to the audition, I was going to be there all the way. Surprisingly, if you knew where to look, there was a lot of support and research online for the subject. Also, fortunately, I could virtually 'talk' to people on various online forums who didn't know who I was or what school I went to about my fears and concerns. I had already mastered the usual time signatures, and was currently working on finesse, confidence, and tricky time signatures as well as messing around with some different salutes. While there were some field commanders out there who had mace work, I was glad that the most I would be expected to wield was a simple baton.

Whether I could believe it or not, the drum major auditions were next week. Tryouts would be every day after school with Ms. Jenkins, our band director, who had been at the school for almost 10 years. As previously mentioned, the marching program hadn't particularly excelled under her, but she managed to keep decent numbers as we had good feeder middle school programs. Two weeks ago, I had covertly picked up the drum major packet which outlined the audition process. I knew we would complete a drill down, conduct a prepared piece, and finally, have some sort of "leadership interview," whatever that meant. For as little as anyone cared about performing, drum major audition always seemed to bring out the competitive side of people. My road to becoming Parktown's other drum major wasn't going to be easy, especially given who I knew I was going to be up against. We weren't the best band in the world, but we had traditions in place that probably used to mean something – you still had to audition to be a section leader, or get a place on the color guard and parts of the drumline. Drum major auditions took place before any of the others, I guess, so that if you didn't make the cut, you could go for something else. As for drum major, from what I could figure, there were going to be five strong contenders – 2 seniors and 3 juniors, not including myself. The others were just underclassmen who wanted the experience of the audition.

After a nervous weekend, in which I basically locked myself in my room to practice, I woke up on Monday morning and calmly selected basics from my wardrobe. The announcement on the band room bulletin board had said candidates should wear lose fitting clothing and comfortable shoes for marching on each of the days. Walking into the familiar halls of Parktown HS, I told Jude to catch a ride home with someone, because I would need to stay after.

"Anything I should know about?" Jude asked, eyebrows raised.

"I'll tell you about it tonight, I promise." I had to at least go to one day of the auditions to know whether or not I had a shot before I discussed the subject with my brother. My twin looked like he wanted to press me, but I distracted him by asking about questions from the only class we shared. Nearing the band room, I wished a good bye to my brother (who made his home in the Commons before the first bell rang) and crept in the familiar door. As I made my way towards my friend Heather, I tried to covertly observe my competition. Of course, there could always be another secret contender like me, but I hoped I had counted up all of who I was going to be up against. Since breaking up with Everett, the percussion room had been off limits, so I joined Heather and the rest of the flute-loops, a section I had been hanging out with since going solo. Initially, they were like, 'why are you here?' but eventually, they got used to my presence and even included me in some of their jokes. Sure, I missed the drumline – the camaraderie, the inside jokes, the friendships, and I won't lie that a small part of me missed Everett...but overall, the flutes were an accepting group and I appreciated their unspoken support.

"So, Heather, I have to tell you something..."

I should probably mention Heather was a bit like Phoebe from Friends, or Luna Lovegood from Harry Potter. One of the many reasons I loved her was because of her crazy spontaneity and overall mellow attitude. I figured me springing on her that I was going to audition this afternoon wouldn't be such a big deal. Some girls might've been upset I hadn't told them this big secret, but Heather usually rolled with whatever life seemed to throw her way, so I wasn't too worried. Her attitude had been especially great when I decided to end things with Everett. I didn't need someone second guessing me, or going all crazy overboard supportive of my decision. I just needed a friend. I think that's why she and I worked so well.

"Is it about what we're having for lunch today? I'm guessing it's mac n' cheese."

I smiled, and answered, "No, not exactly."

"Well, then, what is it?"

I looked around for a moment, but after deciding no one was listening, responded, "I've decided to try out for drum major."

There is a quick moment of silence, before Heather smiled and said, "You'll do great."

I don't think I actually knew how much I needed to hear someone have confidence in me until just that moment. That was another great thing about Heather – somehow, she always knew the right thing to say. All I had to do now was to wait until school was over. The bell rang, and I left to get to Biology. On the way out, I accidently passed by Everett, closer than he usually let me get to him after our break up. Part of me got fluttery and unsettled, but I quickly quashed those feelings. I didn't have room for out of control emotions today. Wistfully, I watched him walk silently away. Although I could have predicted how upset he would be, most of me just wanted my friend back – to tell him about my fears, and ask him if I was crazy for auditioning this afternoon. At the end of the day, Everett was a great listener and for the most part, one of the more mature people I knew. I hoped we would eventually be on speaking terms. We had too much history and I genuinely still cared how things would go for him.

Lost in my thoughts, suddenly, it was after school, and time for me to show up. Walking in the room, I noticed there were a lot more people than I initially anticipated. Nervous thoughts flew through my head – how was I going to beat out all of them? Wondering of I was going to lose before I even started, I made my way cautiously into the room. This first day, I wasn't sure what to think or who to sit next to. The experience was foreign to me, which I had no one to blame but myself. For the past three years, I had mostly hung out with the drumline, or Heather, and all the other wind players seemed to be excluding me a bit. There was a lot of harmless trash talking and inside jokes from the previous season, when finally Ms. Jenkins came out of her office and said, "Alright, let's get started. Those who are here in support of a drum major candidate need to leave."

What can I say? Band members are a supportive group – at least half of the people left the band room and my heart rate slowed down a bit. My mental list of who was auditioning was exactly right.

Pushing her glasses up on her face, Ms. Jenkins looked around the room at us. I instantly sat up straighter. Pushing everything else out of my head, I mentally became the Parktown drum major. Our band director addressed the group, "Okay, I see some new faces here, and that's good. As you're probably aware, upcoming senior Marti Sanchez is returning as drum major and will be helping me with the audition process. Her attitude and help will be noted, and although it is possible, it is unlikely for her to lose her spot. Unfortunately, as you are aware, our other drum major, Jonathan Foster graduated early and will not be available to help us this week. For the rest of you, as we are a small band, I'm going to continue to have only two positions. Today, we will begin with drills. The people who lead this band have to be the best at marching – to help section leaders, to lead by example. I'll see you all out on the black top in five minutes."

Silently, we all moved outside and began stretching. Of all the things that made me nervous about the audition, marching was the highest on the list. In the drumline, we did things a little differently – mainly because there were certain maneuvers that are impossible with a drum attached to your chest. Also, since we didn't have indoor percussion, I didn't have the extra advantage of having marched during the winter season. Plus, drill work is also one of those things that is really difficult to practice on your own. Basically, the drill down put everyone in a block and Marti called out any number of basic and not-so-basic commands, trying to catch us and mess us up. As what I thought would be the weakest part of my audition, I could only hope that everyone was just as out of practice as I was.

If anyone had anything to say about me being at the audition, they didn't speak up, but I did notice a number of raised eyebrows and nudges pointed in my general direction. I had anticipated this reaction, but hoped people wouldn't automatically count me out because of the section I came from. Additionally, I didn't want anyone to believe I wasn't capable of leading the band. They might be surprised, but I was going to show them just how serious I was.

With an intimidating looking clipboard, a whistle around her neck, a stern look on her face and her trademark outdated sunglasses, Ms. Jenkins and said, "Okay, let's form a block. You are on the honor system – if you fail to complete a command in time, then you will drop out. We'll start out with basics."

Our band director nodded to Marti, who blew her whistle, and began clapping out the counts. Her clap was loud, strong, and in time. She was not aggressive, but confident. I didn't think I could be jealous of someone's clapping, but somehow, I was. My classmate called out, "Mark time, mark."

As we began moving our feet, I felt better. This – the intangible knowledge of the downbeat – is what I figured would be my biggest thing. I knew and felt the rhythms better than any of the other candidates. For three years, I was the rhythm. I created the beats.

"Forward march."

We marched a basic block until we ran out of pavement, and Marti had us turn right. Everyone completed the maneuver without missing a step. I was trying desperately not to over think my actions, but to rather just let my body naturally fall in step.

"Back march, hut!"

And so my quest to become the Parktown Pirates drum major began.

Chapter 2: Damn It Feels Good to be a Drum Major

So we back marched, high stepped, about faced, and did all kinds of marching round and round the parking lot. Most of us were rusty, but somehow managed to keep ourselves together. I didn't 'win' per se but I was among the last three standing. Unexpectedly, Todd (a brilliant baritone) and Jenny (a high strung clarinetist) were the last two competing, with Jenny pulling out the overall win on the drill down. Throughout our time on the blacktop, Ms. Jenkins was making notes. I tried not to be nervous, to act like I was supposed to be there.

Afterwards, she announced, "I want to thank everyone for such a great effort this afternoon. Now, it's your turn. I'd like to see each of you call out the commands. Jenny, as the winner, you'll be first and we'll make sure everyone gets a chance after you. Please take the block around the parking lot. Marti, you'll fall in and audition like the rest, and, as with before, if you miss the call, like before, please fall out of the block."

So, one by one, we each had a turn at clapping and calling. Some of the other candidates might have had this experience before during the season or at some point during sectionals, but in drumline we never did any extra marching, and we certainly didn't step out of the bass line to practice calling out "Crabstep, hut!"

Anyway, everything aside, I thought I did okay. My voice was strong, my commands were perfectly in time, and I was able to mess a few people up with my calls. Not used to doing the whole block thing on a regular basis, I had people going back and forth and all over. When I dared look over at Ms. Jenkins, I was pretty sure I saw a smile on her face.

By the time we got through everyone, a good two hours had passed. When the last candidate finished, Ms. Jenkins stepped forward and said, "I'd like to thank everyone again for coming out today. Please check the band room tomorrow morning for your assigned time for tomorrow afternoon to conduct your prepared piece. As the info mentioned, your selection should be less than five minutes, and include both 2/4 and 4/4 time, most preferably a march as well. Please bring your music on CD."

We all nodded.

Our band director finished by saying, "Great job today, kids. Thanks for your effort!"

Unlike a normal practice where everyone socialized for at least twenty minutes afterwards, the group broke up awkwardly and immediately split for their lockers and the student parking lot. Due to the high emotions that were riding on the drum major decision, it wasn't a time to hang out. It was then I realized that somehow in my intense preparation, I had conveniently forgotten that Marti and Jenny were best friends. The two walked towards the parking lot together, leaving me to wonder if my goal to become drum major was really just a dream. I didn't have the inside track, and with the exception of my relationship with Everett, I wasn't the most well known person. Scuffing the ground, I tried to fight my pessimistic feelings. I was buoyed by the realization that if I hadn't at least tried, I would always wonder how things would've turned out.

Driving home in the beat up Volvo station wagon I shared with Jude, I half expected to get a call, or have a text from Everett. Given how rumors could circulate, I'm sure he knew by now I was auditioning. However, the only thing I had missed was a good luck text from Heather.

"I guess I'm doing this on my own," I said to the passing landscape.

At home, I wasn't even two seconds inside the door, when Jude immediately questioned, "Where were you today?"

As I had already hid something from my twin the longest amount of time ever, I responded, "I've decided to try out for drum major."

Although Jude was not a Parktown marching Pirate (he's runs cross country), he knows all about the drama that is my favorite activity.

Eyebrows raised, he asked, "Really?"

I nodded and grabbing a glass from the cupboard, said, "Yes."

One of the many great things about having a twin is that we 'get' each other. I didn't have to go into my many reasons for wanting to audition, or even ask if he supported me, because I knew he would. Twin power!

While I filled the glass full of water and tried to recover some of the fluids I had sweated out over the afternoon, my brother chewed on the sandwich I must've interrupted him eating, before replying, and "Think you have a shot?"

Wiping the excess water from my upper lip, I picked up the other half of his sandwich and answered, "Actually, I do."

"When do you find out?"

"Friday morning."

"Good luck, sis."

"Thanks." I took a bite of the peanut butter and jelly, before I asked, "Can you keep it from Mom and Dad until then?"

"You got it, but why?"

"No sense getting them worked up about something that might not even happen."

"That's no way for the future Parktown drum major to talk, is it?"

I smiled and answered, "Thanks."

Surprisingly, the week went by quicker than I thought it would. In true marching band form, there were rumors and unofficial bets going around who would become the next drum major. Apparently, I was pulling ahead as the dark horse candidate, with Jenny being the obvious choice and perfect match to Marti. Although I had never paid attention during this time of year, I guess everyone else did, and the band room was abuzz with how the auditions had been going. I thought I had done particularly well during my conducting test yesterday and couldn't believe it was my turn to go in next for the interview. Ms. Jenkins had said it would be a 'casual discussion' and that we should 'not be worried.'

"Next."

My band director's voice brought me to the present, and I walked confidently into her office. I had thought a lot about what I was going to say to her, and wasn't sure if she was going to like what I had to say. If I truly deserved to be drum major, it was going to be because I was honest with myself and with the band director. I didn't want to be awarded the role by saying what I thought she wanted to hear. This band deserved better.

"Have a seat, Rigby."

I sat in one of the uncomfortable mismatched chairs across from Ms. Jenkins' desk in her cluttered office. Surrounded by broken and old instruments, pictures from countless seasons, and pages of sheet music it was a comfortable place. I would have felt more at home in the percussion room, but this was a close second.

I should probably mention, for everyone who had been in the Parktown band for more than half a day, knew Ms. Jenkins liked to talk. In fact, that was I why I wasn't as nervous – I imagined most of the 'interview' would be a chance for her to just do what she loved best – talk.

Taking a deep breath and leaning back in her big leather chair, she started with, what I guessed would be a long winded set of opening remarks, "Well, Ms. Sullivan, I have to admit, I'm honestly surprised at your intentions. I know you've been a strong member of the drumline for the past three seasons, and I didn't realize you had any intention of trying for drum major. What changed your mind?"

Surprised to be speaking so soon, I took a deep breath and answered honestly, "Ms. Jenkins, I'm sure you would agree with me if I say that there is a lot of room for improvement in this band."

She nodded, so I continued, "Listen, I know I might not be the logical choice. I don't have the experience everyone else has, I'm not as talented as they are and I'm certainly not going to give you the answer that probably everyone else who has sat in this chair has given you about their leadership qualities. Instead, I'm going to tell you that this band, more than anything, needs someone to kick its ass. I think we have a lot of great things going for us – you obviously care a lot about the band and we have some true talent, but I think with the right person in charge, we could really go somewhere this season."

Deciding I should probably quit while I was ahead, I finished by saying, "What I want you to know is, I've thought about it, and I believe I am the right person for the change. I know I won't be popular or maybe even liked, but I will be remembered and that will be enough for me."

Ms. Jenkins sat still a moment. I wasn't sure what else was even on her list of questions to ask. This could very well be the shortest drum major interview ever conducted.

Finally, she responded, "And you're sure you're willing to do whatever it takes?"

Definitely not the answer I was expecting. I stumbled for a moment, before looking her directly in the eyes and answering, "Whatever it takes."

"Thanks for coming in, Rigby. Your answer was...refreshing. As you are aware, the results will be posted tomorrow after school. Whoever is selected drum major will be expected to play a role in the section leader auditions next week, as well as the junior high orientation week."

"Thanks for your time, Ms. Jenkins."

I walked out of the office in a trance. Had I really just told Ms. J I would kick the collective band's ass?! And what the hell did 'refreshing' mean? What couldn't I just keep my big mouth shut? Devastated I had obviously just written off any chance I had been working towards, my head hung down and I sighed deeply. Why would our band director choose the girl who thinks the band sucks, when she could have perfect Jenny and Marti? Their obvious closeness and chemistry had only grown during the week, and I was sure all of the candidates could already picture them in their perfect matching sparkly drum majorette uniforms. There wasn't a place for me on the drum major podium.

Sadly, I walked out to the parking lot behind the school where we had managed to get a spot that morning. It was then I noticed one of the only cars left in the lot was a familiar white Taurus with faded Ludwig stickers.

Everett.

I heard gravel crunch behind me and sensed a familiar presence – one I had been expecting since I started the week. As Everett approached, I was reminded we hadn't been alone – truly alone – except for a handful of times since the break up. If I was honest with myself, that even though I knew ending our relationship was the right thing, sometimes I second guessed my decision. It would've been so easy just to keep on dating him through our senior year. I'd always have a date for everything, my parents more or less liked him, and we photographed well together – all of which were terrible reasons to continue dating someone.

"Why didn't you tell me?" I knew his tone. He was trying to keep the bitterness and hurt out of his voice. I tried to remind myself of the reason he was speaking that way. I was the one at fault. I had put the sadness in his voice.

"I don't know," I answered honestly.

"I wouldn't have told anyone."

"I know."

I didn't think Everett wanted to hear that in the case of my audition, the choice to try out was something I needed to do, on my own. If I had told him, it would've made it not my own, which would've totally defeated the purpose.

"Do you not like our section?"

I sighed and answered, "That's not it at all. In fact, that has nothing to do with my decision."

He paused before replying, "Ever since we broke up, I guess I feel like I don't know you anymore."

"You're the one who's made it that way. I've tried to give you your space, tried to respect whatever it was you needed. Look, Ev, this is my first break up too. I don't know what I'm doing." Rather desperate to move the conversation away from our past relationship, I asked, "If Jenkins somehow chooses me, would you actually follow me as drum major?"

To complete the mass overhaul the band needed, it was going to need the full support of every section, and probably most importantly the drumline captain.

Everett trudged around a minute before he replied, "I honestly don't know."

"If Jenkins does pick me, Ev, I want to shake things up. I don't want to talk about a good season and then not follow through. I want to be a winner this year."

"Fine, I'll think about it. But what if she doesn't pick you?"

For the past couple of weeks, I had been so focused on the auditions, I didn't think about what would happen after. If I wasn't drum major, the thought of the same old routine in the Line wasn't that exciting to me. I couldn't imagine not marching, but at the same time, why would I want to do it if it was just going to be another losing season?

Hopefully, I wouldn't be forced to make that kind of decision.

I shrugged, and finally answered, "I don't know."

Everett backed away and headed towards his car, saying, "Later, Riggles."

The endearment was his old nickname for me, a forgotten memento from our freshman year. He used it so often that year, the name had stuck and it was how most everyone on the Line referred to me. I'm sure the moniker was just something that slipped out, unintentionally and not anything more significant. To make him feel better, I responded, "See ya, Mount Everett."

I didn't even bother try to concentrate during class the next day. Fortunately, I didn't need to, because hey, when your twin brother is the class valedictorian, you always have someone to explain things to you. I wasn't sure why Ms. Jenkins was going to wait until after school, but I had to respect her decision. Throughout the day, I thought of my collective audition, of what I had said and still believed, perhaps naively, that I still had a chance.

When the final bell rang, I was torn between wanting to sprint down to the band room and not wanting to go at all. I wished there was some way to find out without everyone else watching. Still, deep down, I knew a drum major wouldn't run from something like this. A true leader would face the music.

I could only hope I reached the list before anyone else did.

As I neared the band room, it appeared the reality of the situation was not going to happen. Naturally, and just my luck, there was a band class the last period of the day, and of course they were all hanging around to see what the final decision was going to be.

Gathering my courage, I took my time walking the final length of the hall. If Ms. Jenkins wanted a change, she would pick me. If not, it wasn't meant to be. I tried to keep that thought in mind as I opened the door and walked into the band room. Everything else was blocked out as I walked up to the list.

Two names.

One of them was mine.

Strangely, the other one was not Marti's.

Chapter 3: You Say You Want a Revolution

I looked at the names again: Rigby Sullivan and Jennifer Chen.

Was I missing something? Was Ms. Jenkins going to add a third drum major? I knew Marti's audition hadn't been perfect, but not seeing her name was a complete surprise.

Apparently, a hush had fallen over the room as I had approached the list, because when I looked up, everyone was doing their best to look at me, but pretend like they weren't. Conversations had become quiet and it seemed the group collectively leaned in to see what I would do. I was trying to process what I had read. Ms. Jenkins had thrown not one, but two curveballs by making Jenny and me leaders of the band.

What would Marti do?

What would Jenny say?

Why did Ms. Jenkins do what she did?

How would everyone react?

Wait, why was I worrying about everyone else? I was DRUM MAJOR!!!

So I did what I do when I'm in an exceptionally good mood, I whooped! My crazy recognizable yell (long story, short, it's a family tradition that goes back generations) seemed to release the tension in the room, and, after a big group laugh, members of the marching Pirates came up to start congratulating me. I hadn't realized I had as much support as I did in the band, and I found myself getting choked up. Basically, there was simply too much emotion going on in a matter of minutes for me to comprehend.

While I was talking to everyone about how excited I was, I realized I hadn't seen either Jenny or Marti yet, and for that I was very glad. It wasn't that I liked or disliked either of my fellow juniors, it was just I needed some time to settle down from the news. Did I think Jenny and I would make a good conducting team? She wouldn't have been my top choice, but I was sure we could make it work. How would Jenny take directing with me? Sure, I wasn't her best friend, but maybe together we could make something out of the Parktown program.

"WHAT THE HELL?!" A shout from a recognizable voice sounded out across the room (and to be honest, I was paraphrasing a bit).

I guessed they found the list. Rather than be calm, understanding, young adults about Ms. Jenkins' decision, I had a feeling things were about to take a very opposite turn.

Taking a deep breath, I approached my classmates and decided to open with, "Hey, Jenny, congratulations!"

My co-drum major turned around, recognized who I was and said rudely, "What the hell is that supposed to mean?!"

I shrugged and answered, "Umm, I don't know, I guess I mean, 'good job.' I'm really looking forward to—"

"To what? To our magical season together? To all the good times we're going to have? I can't believe

Jenkins would pull this crap. If Marti isn't drum major, then I don't want to be either."

Wait, was she threatening to drop out because of her friend not being her perfect co-Drum major? I instantly become equal parts angry and sad. She was supposed to be the best of the best? The leader of the band? I would rather lead the group by myself than have someone like her conducting anywhere near me. In my life pre-being selected as drum major (yeah, I know that was only 10 minutes ago), I wasn't one to rock the boat. It wasn't my style. I had been content to be in the background, happy to be part of Everett and Rigby. However, the thought occurred to me that it was going to be my name called when we went to competitions in the fall, and I sure didn't want that kind of attitude near me or my band.

"Then why don't you?" I asked.

"Why don't I what?" Jenny huffed.

"Why don't you quit?"

Jenny stared me down for a minute, trying to figure out if I was for real or not.

"Maybe I will," she huffed.

I put my hands on my hips and said, "Well, if you're going to bring that attitude, then you'd be doing everyone a favor by quitting. Whether or not you're with us, we're going somewhere this season!"

"Fine!"

Of course, being in the band room, we had already drawn a small crowd. Thus far, we weren't exactly stating the strongest case for 'Team Parktown Drum Major,' but I wasn't going to back down. I honestly believed what I had said. There wasn't going to be room in my band for her attitude and everyone should know my feelings on the subject as soon as possible. It was only then I noticed Marti had taken the opportunity to slink away during Jenny and I's 'discussion.'

Ms. Jenkins, unaware of the drama that had been going on right outside her door, came out, and said,

"Hello, girls, congratulations to both of you! I look forward to what we're going to accomplish this season."

"Thank you, I won't let you down!" I said firmly.

"I quit!" said Jenny at the same time.

Ms. Jenkins blinked rapidly, and then asked, "Can I speak to both of you in my office?"

Trying not to glare at each other, we followed her. It took a lot to ruffle Ms. Jenkins' feathers and she had to know what was going to happen when she posted the results. Our band director was a lot of things, but stupid was not one of them. I sat calmly in one of the chairs, while Jenny flounced into her seat.

"Jenny, would you care to explain yourself?"

"What about Marti?"

I tried to control my breathing. Ultimately, I couldn't blame my classmate for how she was acting. Jenny was trying to stick up for her best friends and loyalty was not something I would ever fault. What I didn't like, however, was immaturity.

"What about her?" Ms. Jenkins wisely turned the question around.

"I thought... We thought..."

"I'm sorry you are frustrated with my decision. Although I do not see a need to, I would be happy to show you how I came to this conclusion. The scoring was close, but ultimately you and Rigby came out on top." Her voice lowered and she asked, "Is this something you want to do, Jenny?"

She looked at me, then looked back at our band director and said, "Yes, it is."

Jenny collected her things and left the room. Ms. Jenkins and I both sat in shock. Something shifted in me. While before, perhaps I had been a bit intimidated of our band director, I now felt I was close to her equal. Sure, I had no real control or ability to discipline, but I wanted Ms. Jenkins to know she had made the right decision in choosing me. I was the first to find my voice and said brightly, "That's okay – better she backs out now than halfway through the season."

"I can go to the next candidate..." her voice trailed away.

"Let me guess? Marti?"

"Yes."

"And the next?

"It doesn't matter." Ms. Jenkins straightened up and said, "Why don't we look at the score. I think it's something one person can do. Does that sound good?"

In her question, the reality of the situation sunk in. I was going to be the sole drum major for Parktown. I would have no one else to blame if things went wrong. Suddenly, my inner optimist must have grabbed hold of the situation, because it occurred to me that when we won, which we would, I would be the one to take the credit. For the first time in my high school career, I would have a chance to do something on my own – not as someone's girlfriend or someone's twin, just me, Rigby Sullivan.

"Are you sure you can handle this?" Ms. Jenkins nudged gently.

"I am."

"Great – because I have some wonderful news!"

I was surprised that a) Ms. J had readily accepted my statement I could lead the band completely on my own, but also b) she was down half of his drum major staff and that fact didn't seem to bother her. Still stunned by the events of the past half-hour, I could only reply dumbly, "What's that?"

"I'm not sure if you heard, but we finally got money in the budget for some help for the fall season. Just today I got confirmation that we're getting an instructor!"

"That's great," I replied, breathing a sigh of relief. After Jenny's (and probably Marti's) defection from the band, the announcement was definitely wonderful news I needed to keep me sane. As confident as I was in myself, having additional help could only help us improve.

"Not only is he going to help us with band camp, he's agreed to stay on and act as an overall support person throughout the season. He comes highly recommended from working and marching with some of the top drum corps in the country. I think we're really lucky to get him."

I was a bit stunned. Usually, our 'support' was in the form of local music majors and alumni who took pity on us to come for a few days to help us with our lame excuse for a band camp. They would check in on us now and then, but we rarely saw any of them past September. As I mentioned, we weren't a good band and outside of some overenthusiastic band parents, we didn't have a lot of support. We never knew anyone with drum corps experience, mostly because we couldn't afford their type of help. Suddenly, my mind was reeling with the potential for our future season. However, at that moment, I couldn't think of a single thing to ask except, "What's his name?"

"Ned Buchanan."

"Ned?" I tried very hard to keep the skepticism out of my voice, but was entirely unsuccessful. I wondered what kind of confidence a wannabe band director this so call character named Ned could inspire in our band.

"He comes very highly recommended, Rigby, I don't think we should judge him based on his name."

I tried to ignore my own immaturity by changing the subject and asked, "When do we get to meet him?"

"Not until band camp. He has previous commitments until then. Actually, we're very lucky to get him. He's a music education student from—"

"I can imagine," I interrupted.

One of the premiere music education programs wasn't that far from us. Given the reputation of our program, we hadn't seen any of the students come and help us. Most people could recognize a lost cause when they saw one. Furthermore, I was relieved. As excited as I was to have good ole Ned's help, I desperately wanted a chance to get everyone into shape before Mr. High and Mighty Corps Man showed up to judge us and find us hopelessly unworthy. Hoping to steer the conversation away from Ned, I asked, "So, now that I'm drum major, I have to know, what's the theme of the show this year?"

"Ned and I decided on a great theme – Around the World in 8 Minutes!" she exclaimed excitedly.

While I was glad Ms. Jenkins was excited about the show, I kind of didn't like how seamlessly Ned had already worked his way into our band without even setting foot on campus. Still, the concept already sounded like a more original show than we had done in all my previous seasons. Usually, we did boring crowd pleasers that were easy to memorize and didn't have complicated parts. I was already picturing where we could go with music. Not even sure what the arrangement was, I was cautiously optimistic. Perhaps we'd finally get a show that could take us places.

"That sounds amazing – I can't wait."

Coming down off the high I had been on since reading my name, I excused myself from Ms. Jenkins' office and walked out into the now deserted band room. Having been locked up with the band director, I wasn't sure if or what Jenny had told everyone about her decision to quit. Furthermore, I wasn't sure how the rest of the band was going to react. Both Jenny and Marti were popular marching Pirates, and while I completely disagreed with their immaturity, I hoped after awhile they would decide to come back as musicians. We needed strong players. I hoped no one would follow their lead – I needed everyone I could get!

"So?"

I had resisted texting Jude on the way home, determined to tell him the news in person. I smiled, because my brother had obviously been waiting for me to pull into our drive and all but attacked me as soon as I opened the car door.

"So, what?"

"Did you get it or not?"

"I certainly did. High five?"

"Definitely."

We proceeded to go through the motions of a part handshake, part choreographed routine of an extended high five tradition we had started when we were younger. The action was reserved for only the most exciting of events. After finishing, Jude helped bring in my various bags and said, "What happens next?"

"What happens is..." My voice drifted off.

"Rigby?"

I cleared my throat and said, "What happens is, I get people into shape. On my own."

"What do you mean? I thought there were two of you."

"There was."

"And?"

"And now there is just me."

"What happened?"

I knew Jude was easily bored by the inner workings and nearly constant drama of the band. In the world of his cross country team, it basically came down to who was the fastest. The only thing that kept his life interesting was practicing with the girl's team.

"Marti—"

"Sanchez?"

"Yes."

As if recalling a particularly fond memory, he said, "Go on."

I narrowed my eyebrows and said, "You didn't."

"You were late when I was picking you up one time."

"Is there any girl in the school you haven't made out with?"

"Some sophomores and a few of the senior class ladies. Anyway, what about you? Are you ready to direct by yourself?"

The unspoken question, the character trait I had been fighting – that of always being supported by someone was there. Trying to believe the words, I said, "I'm ready to at least give it a try."

"How about telling Mom and Dad, are you up for there?"

After thinking all I had been through in the past week, telling my parents was going to be the easy part. As we walked to the house, I asked, "Do you think they'll be mad I kept them in the dark?"

Thankfully, my parents were only a little mad I had kept such a big decision from them. We celebrated over the weekend and even made a special online purchase (with rush order) for drum major gloves and a fancy whistle for my new role. Even though I had finals to study for, I was more interested in the week ahead. The Parktown marching Pirates would simultaneously be working with the middle school students coming up and holding auditions for section leadership. I wasn't sure if there would be any further fallout from the drama of Friday afternoon. Did Marti and Jenny have enough influence in the band to take people with them? Would they change their minds and rejoin? And what about the other competitors? How would they take my placement?

In the end, it turned out my worries were all unfounded. Marti and Jenny left the band and no one followed them. While I would admit having someone next to me who had done this before would've made my life easier, I was ready to tackle the challenge of solo field command. There was gossip around their decision, but I was silent on the subject. I wanted to leave the door open if they ever wanted to rejoin us. Furthermore, I was too busy to worry about much else. During the week, in my duties as drum major and without a co-drum major, I was running around trying to be everywhere at once. I'm not saying Marti and Jonathan weren't 'there' for us exactly, but they were usually more interested in flirting each other than the rest of the band as a general rule. Rather than being constantly distracted by someone else, I wanted to make sure people knew who I was and that I put them and the band first. Furthermore, I hoped that if I showed boundless energy and constant 'band spirit' that maybe my enthusiasm would catch on.

At the same time that section leader auditions were going on, the color guard auditions were going on at the same time, and I wanted to make my presence known with the girls and token guy, a lovely sophomore by the name of Tommy. Based on seniority and motivation level, Adelaide, another junior, was running the auditions and was most likely going to be color guard captain. She and I got along okay, but I knew this was going to be a sticky relationship. As bad as we were as instrumentalists and marchers, the color guard was also spectacularly bad. I wasn't sure how I was going to address this specific problem just yet – especially given the fact I knew literally nothing about the guard except what I had heard on judges' tapes – repeatedly – from previous years. Most of the girls seemed content to wear some sequins, dance around the field, and not put any particular emphasis on timing or choreography. I knew the transition was going to be an uphill battle. The need for change also brought forward the fact I was totally intimidated by any section where I couldn't 'do' what they were doing. It's not like I could pick up a flag and be all, 'Oh, here's how you do it.' Nor could I pick up a flute or trumpet and blast out the part. At the same time, a good leader could overcome anything – at least, that's what I would keep telling myself. At the minimum, I would lead by example. Attitude had to count for something, right?

For the rest of the week, Ms. Jenkins and I had our work cut out for us to decide on the leadership for the marching band. My selection for drum major apparently made things okay to have the door opened for anyone else who was a bit...different. Although I had never been to the section leader auditions, this year seemed particularly strange. Based on how what I had seen of him at the drum major audition, it seemed Todd would make an excellent brass captain, but I wasn't sure who would be his woodwind equivalent. With Jenny gone, it seemed there was no natural person to take her place...until a surprise turned up in the form of a freshman saxophonist named Emma. I had never met anyone with so much natural leadership ability. People just listened to her. Everett, was, of course, unchallenged for the role of drumline captain.

Sitting in her office on Thursday afternoon, Ms. Jenkins and I discussed all of the candidates and their various strengths and weaknesses. Even though I had my reservations about my relationship with my ex-boyfriend and how we would work together, my band director and I completely agreed on Everett and Todd. Todd was the strong, strong silent type, an outstanding player, an excellent marcher, and just an overall intimidating guy. He could keep people in line. Furthermore, I didn't sense he was carrying a grudge from not winning drum major, which was a good thing.

However, we were about to come to fists over who would lead the woodwinds. Ms. Jenkins was fighting for Kristin, who was going to be a senior, but, to me at least, didn't embody the band spirit I thought she should have. She wanted to be in charge, but I think mostly to save face because everyone thought she should be in charge. De facto leadership was not something I had room for in my dream band. I didn't care if it was unorthodox to put a sophomore in the role. Emma was the best person for the job.

Ms. Jenkins sighed, and for at least the hundredth time this week, said, "I wish Ned was here..."

I personally didn't see what Ned being here with us would accomplish. We knew the abilities of the members of the band, not some random instructor who hadn't grown up with the band. However, I guessed, it would be nice to have a third person to break the tie.

I decided to make my final case and said, "Here's what I see, Ms. Jenkins. Let's make Emma woodwind captain, and give Kristin the lieutenant position."

Technically, we'd never even had a lieutenant position before (and captains really only applied to the drumline and color guard). People kind of just worked things out in an informal way, and unless there was some sort of personality conflict, there was no official designation. However, I knew other bands had dedicated systems in place – a chain of command and someone to be truly responsible for the others in their section. Maybe the extra structure could help our program as well. Fortunately, I didn't have to resort to tears, and in the end, got my way. Ms. Jenkins was hesitant, but accepted my advice.

Once the list was printed and ready for the band room wall, I knew my next step was talking to the new leaders. I had ideas and plans for the summer, and I needed their help.

"Ms. Jenkins?" I asked as she walked to the door.

"Yes?"

"Before you post it – can I call a band leadership meeting after school tomorrow?"

"I don't see why not."

I scribbled a hasty note on the list and watched as the Parktown band director posted the list that would hopefully impact people's lives the way it had mine.

Chapter 4: Summer Backslide

"So, you probably know why I've called you here today…" I let my voice drift away, desperately hoping someone would jump in.

I received blank stares from everyone except Emma, who was grinning like an idiot. Looking at her obvious enthusiasm, I couldn't help but smile back at her. I continued, "Okay, maybe you don't know why I called a meeting today. First of all, let me personally say congratulations to all of you – Ms. Jenkins and I are confident that you will help us shake things up in the Parktown Pirate marching band and make this a season we can all remember."

I let my introduction rest. This was it. This was the point where I had to lay all my cards on the table. I took a deep breath and continued, "I'm not going to shy away from it guys, the fact is, we currently suck."

I paused for a moment to see if anyone would argue, but there was none. Well, at least we were all on the same page. Of course, I had to recognize there was a fine line between apathy and understanding. Too enthused by my own emotion, I started pacing the band room floor and said, "I don't know about the rest of you, but I'm kind of sick of the current activity we call 'marching.' I'm sick of losing, of sloppy playing and marching, of being laughed at or ignored by every other school we come across. That's the reason I auditioned for drum major and I think, or, at least I hope, that's why Jenkins gave me the position. Look, I know we've got all the elements to make a good band, we just haven't been using them. So, I figured that's at least one thing we have on our side. All the other bands in our district don't have a lot of room to move, but I believe we can surprise everyone with our improvement."

I risked a look up, and was greeted by some smiles and nods. Finally – a reaction!

Feeling I was gaining momentum, I added, "But here's the thing, I can't do it on my own. If we're going to shake things up and actually win or place at a competition or two, the change is going to have to come from all the leadership and that could mean people not liking us. It could mean long hours in the sun. It could mean a lot of things we're not used to. And what I want to know is, are you with me? If things are going to change, we can't just talk about it, I'm going to need the leadership to help me act on these things."

I looked around the room, desperately hoping I would get a verbal 'second' from someone. All I heard was deafening silence. Was it possible my dreams were about to be crushed this early in the season? That my expectations would be wrecked before I even had a chance to try?

My hero came from where I least expected it. Everett replied, "The drumline is behind you. We'll do whatever it takes."

With someone having broken the ice, Emma chirped, "I'll make sure the woodwinds are, too!"

Todd added, "Don't worry about the brass."

We all looked at Adelaide. By far, she wasn't the sharpest tool in the shed. However, she did have a great deal of natural ability with the flags.

Realizing we were all waiting for an answer, she said brightly, "Oh, right...um, I'll do whatever I can with the guard."

Although small, it was a start I could do something with. While I wished everyone could match my own level of enthusiasm, I had to recognize this level of change would take time.

Crossing my arms, I continued, "Okay then, our new 'attitude' starts now. In addition to what we've just gone through with the upcoming freshman, I thought about holding a small mini-camp in between Finals and graduation. Kind of a refresher for everyone. It won't be mandatory, but I would encourage you to encourage your sections that it's something they would be interested. After that, depending on everyone's vacation and work schedules, I was thinking about setting up random sectionals one day a week – a time for people to check in and work on fundamentals and the boring stuff, so that once we get the score for the show, we won't have to waste a month remembering how to play our instruments. What do you say?"

"If Jenkins will open the school, then we'll be there," Todd answered.

And so, we adopted my plans. And surprisingly, we stuck to them. While I said additional meetings and practices were 'voluntary,' we actually got a decent turnout out of people over the summer. The numbers waxed and waned, but overall I think I saw almost every member of the band come through one of our extra practices. Without anything else to go on, I went back to basics, and even though we didn't have the drill for the show or the final musical arrangements, we went over scales and tuning and correct posture and rolling our steps. The extra practices were also good for me, as I became super comfortable conducting the band. Towards the end of July, there was a bit of confidence starting to show on everyone's faces. In previous seasons, we were always laughing at ourselves, never holding attention or standing up straight. I thought back to our behavior and wondered how we were even able to get through an eight minute show. Although I couldn't speak for everyone, I knew there had been times when slacking off had been fun, but this new sense of accomplishment felt much better.

I had even managed to get through to Adelaide. One day, early in the summer, I decided to be a bit sneaky. After growing frustrated witnessing the group, once again, prancing around the field with no particular direction, rather than actually practice any set routine or block with their flags, I wandered up and requested, "Teach me."

There was an immediate spark of interest from the four girls who were actually there. I had to admit, flag work was more difficult than it looked, and I barely had the patience to spend most of the afternoon to master a simple spin. Gritting my teeth, and knowing this was for the best of the band, I asked politely, "Could you put together a routine that would help me practice?"

Adelaide looked at me as if I was crazy for a minute wanting to learn a skill I would have no real use for, but then, in her bubbly voice, answered, "Sure!"

My hope was the 'help' she was going to give me would turn into a set of basics she could use with the rest of the section. The color guard seemed to be lacking what musicians had naturally – scales and rudiments. Over the next week, while I acquired a pretty decent set of basic color guard skills, a warm up set of movements was formed. As much progress as we made, I wondered idly, would Ned really be able to help this section come the fall season? I had all but forgotten we were even going to get help in less than a month's time. We had already come so far, I almost wondered if we even needed this guy's help. Of course, he would be able to polish the group, but I didn't want him to interfere with our new found confidence. Although I appreciated everyone's hard work, I knew the slightest imbalance could send us downhill back to where we had been.

In this manner, the summer passed quickly and my constant marching activity had a totally unexpected personal bonus. While I'd never had body image problems, I wouldn't have ever exactly classified myself as extremely 'healthy' or 'fit' until now. From May, I had dropped four sizes and with all my hours in the sun, had been bronzed to a very flattering color (even if I had obvious tan lines). My arms were wonderfully toned from the conducting and my hair had pretty blonde streaks in it. When I passed by myself in the mirror, I almost didn't recognize myself. I began to wonder why I hadn't auditioned for drum major years ago.

As my the start of my senior year came neared, I was in a further great mood because Ms. Jenkins was finally going to pass out the music. Tomorrow would be the first of our official pre-band camps. We would have one week of trying to learn the music and maybe even taking a shot at the drill, before the great Ned Sullivan joined us. I looked back on the summer with a lot of pride. While we weren't the best in the region or state or probably even school district, we were definitely the best Parktown had ever been. Surprisingly, I owed a lot of the improvements to the underclassmen. When we first started things, I fully anticipated the upperclassmen to pick up the slack, and quite honestly, was even harder on the little ninth and tenth graders. To my delight, the underclassmen worked harder. I'm not sure if it was a weird connection or allegiance to Emma, but whatever the reason, they were the true force behind our continued improvement.

As I reflected on the past months, I wondered if I hadn't missed out on my last real summer. Next year at this time, if everything worked out I would hopefully be employed and putting away money for college. Unlike my brother, who practically lived and breathed summer romances (his job as a lifeguard made it easy work), I wasn't the type to have some sort of summer fling. Watching Jude get wrapped up in texting sessions or having to watch as he inevitably turned up to breakfast with yet another hickey, part of me wished I'd found someone to steal a few moments with over the summer. An unexpected result of the ongoing sectionals was the constant flirting and summer romances that had blossomed among various Parktown band members. I had been surrounded by lovey dovey and overly dramatic teenagers all summer. I had been a shoulder to cry on and on more than one occasion, the friend left behind while someone more interesting entered the picture.

It's not that I was completely without a chance of my own summer loving either...

Although avoiding him had been difficult, I had resisted the stares and appreciative glances from Everett all summer. Our paths hadn't crossed that much. He promised me he would take care of the drumline and I was content to believe him. They mostly practiced separately from the rest of us, and that fact was fine by me – I had enough going on with just the band. I'm not sure if it was the fact I had been too long without any male companionship, or just that Everett and I were a good fit together, but I was starting to wonder why I had broken up with him in the first place. At the very end of practice, he had asked to meet up with me at 'our place' later tonight under the pretense of talking about my old section.

Even though I wouldn't admit it, I did dress more carefully than I usually would o meet Everett. With all my weight loss, I had more to choose from. My mom, really proud of not only my drum majorness, but also my commitment, had noticed I had to belt everything up, and last week had taken me on a bit of a shopping spree. While I wanted to get mostly work out and warm up clothes for practice, my mom forced me to buy a few other things I could wear at school. Tonight, I was glad she had talked me into a cute sundress.

I suggested to Everett that we meet up, rather than him picking me up. I figured if I could just make it to the start of the school year, then maybe I would be able to escape the backslide straight into my ex-boyfriend's arms. We had been moving towards friendship, but there were moments of weakness on both of our sides, and a new flirtation had started that I wasn't entirely comfortable with. I knew myself, and I knew if I wasn't careful I was going to end up back in his strong arms. It hadn't gone without notice that he had thus far avoided advances from a number of interested young ladies in the Parktown community. Part of me was slightly flattered, but also nervous. Did he think we had a chance of getting back together?

Checking my reflection in the rear view mirror, I looked at myself and tried to remind myself this was just a dinner between two friends. Everett was waiting for me inside the local Chipotle. We small talked throughout the meal, just like old times. Ev caught me up with all the developments and gossip of my old section. It wasn't until Everett walked me to my car that I realized we hadn't talked about why he had invited me out today.

"So, what's up?" I asked.

He shrugged a moment before replying, "Honestly, at the beginning of the summer I wasn't sure how things were going to go between us..."

"Neither was I."

"And, I thought you should know how proud we are of you."

"We?" I asked flirtatiously, eyebrows lifted.

"Okay, I'll admit, me too. I only wish we had all started caring a few seasons ago."

I nodded, and said "Totally, but since we didn't, we have to make this one count, don't we?"

Everett was quiet a long moment before he answered, "About that..."

And then my ex-boyfriend, out of nowhere, leaned in for a kiss. My body, so used to responding to his, moved forward to meet his familiar lips, until I abruptly stopped the embrace at the last second.

What was I doing?

What was he doing? This wasn't what I wanted, was it? I ended up awkwardly burrowing my head into Everett's shoulder. I didn't want to face him. I had completely just shut his advance down. I was mortified.

I backed away slowly and said quietly, "I can't, Everett, I'm sorry."

Without another word, I hurried into my car, and sped away as fast as possible, wondering if I had done the right thing. Raising the volume and trying to drown out the incident, I was unsuccessful and relived the horrible cringe-worthy moment the entire drive home. I debated calling Heather, then about whether I should tell Jude, but couldn't actually bring myself to share with anyone what had transpired. I wanted to put the embarrassing moment behind me and pretend like it never happened. Had I been sending out mixed signals? I thought I had been clearly platonic throughout the summer, but maybe I was wrong.

The following day, with the whole band gathered, Ms. Jenkins went into a long speech about the coming season and all the influences for the pieces, effectively putting everyone to sleep. Her extended speech gave me even more time to dwell on my actions with Everett, who was now effectively pretending like I didn't exist. In the end, even after a fitful night sleep, I still felt like I had done the right thing. Leading Everett on, simply because he was there and we had a history wasn't going to help anyone – not me, not the Line, not the rest of the band. Still, as proud as I was of myself for withholding, I had to wonder what or who I was waiting for. As far I could tell, Ev was my only real potential for action and was I prepared to turn into a nun for my senior year? Maybe I could put that extra energy into being drum major. Maybe that was the solution. Coming out of my muddled thoughts, my band director was finally finishing, I clapped my hands together for attention. Deciding the first response was definitely not loud enough, I looked seriously around my gathered band and clapped again, louder and harder, all but shouting, "Band, ten HUT!"

"HUT!!!!!"

Ms. Jenkins looked a bit surprised, then said, "Okay, I'll let Rigby take it from here."

Pushing stray thoughts of Everett firmly aside, I stood up proudly and projected my voice so the 60 instrumentalists and 20 color guard members could hear me, "Okay gang, let's break out into sections and start going over the music. Take it at a slow tempo. I'm going to check in on each of your sections throughout the day. Remember how we practiced this summer. This is nothing to get worried about. Attack the music, play with confidence and then we'll worry about how it all comes together. We want to show Mr. Buchanan when he arrives that he's got a winning band to work with."

Chapter 5: Hey North! Hey What?
Introduce Yourself.

Pre-band camp practices went both better and worse than I had expected. The band, well, at least the brass and woodwinds, were taking like little ducklings to water with the music. I couldn't believe how far they had come in such a short time. Unfortunately, the drumline and the color guard were another matter entirely. Everett seemed to be taking my rejection of his kiss by not only ignoring me, but also pretty much causing the Line to act up every time the entire band assembled. With the percussionists slacking, the color guard quickly followed and, in record time, was back to their usual undisciplined selves. Needless to say, this behavior severely cramped the progress I thought we would make during the week. The band I had worked towards during the summer was no longer present, and part of me felt like a failure. I knew the lack of progress wasn't my fault, it was more about Everett's immaturity than anything else, but I couldn't help feeling down. The amazing and fantastic Ned was going to show up tomorrow, and by judging the band, it was going to be like he was judging me. I knew my thoughts were silly and it was still very early in the season, but I couldn't help feeling the way I did.

At the end of practice, Heather, my voice reason, asked, "So, explain to me again, how is it your fault if things go wrong?"

"I've been in charge of them all summer. I don't want Ned to think I'm a completely incompetent drum major."

"He won't. I know it's not exactly the same, but didn't you tell me he's seen where we were last season via video? I'm sure, with all his experience, he'll figure out where all the trouble is coming from. Plus, he's just one dude, who cares what he thinks? Everyone knows how far you've brought us. They trust you."

I wanted Heather's words to make me feel better, but I was more anxious than ever. In addition to the drumline and their constant screwing around, I had serious doubts my former section had managed to memorize any of the part which Ned had written for them. The stupid thing was, I was too irritated with Everett to go over and set the drummers straight. While I told myself my lack of response was because I was too busy dealing with the rest of the band, deep down I knew it was because I had no urge to face Everett. I didn't want to deal with the confrontation or awkwardness.

Ms. Jenkins had suggested Ned meet us separately before the rest of the band, and given the lack of progress we'd made during the week, I completely agreed. I wanted a chance to try and explain myself before he saw us in action. I tried not to be nervous, but, again, I couldn't help my feelings. I had no idea what this Ned guy was going to be like or how he was going to treat me or the rest of the band. Gathering my confidence and trying to focus on the positives I walked into the deserted band room...and, as usual, I had beaten my band director in. When I was earlier than her, I usually headed straight into the percussion room. I would release some tension by noodling around on the drums for a few minutes and usually feel better. When I finished beating out my frustrations onto a Real Feel pad, I heard someone outside in the band room – someone who was obviously in the middle of a very personal phone call.

"...I told you – I was going to come here. My decision is final."

The caller – a male – waited for awhile, and kept trying to talk, but gave up and listened for a few minutes before finally responding, "We're not having this conversation, Denise, I've made my decision – please, just forget I existed – I can't keep doing this... "

There was a sound of a phone shutting and a deep sigh.

At that moment, I was torn. I sensed whoever was out there could use someone to listen to, however, maybe that person just wanted to be by alone for a moment to sort themselves out. After a few moments, I hesitantly asked, "Hello?"

"Hello?" a deep tenor voice answered back.

I wandered out from the smaller room and almost collided with the stranger. Straightening myself, I got a look at him and found myself faced with the hottest guy I had ever seen. He had dark hair, closely cropped. He was standing casually, holding a motorcycle helmet under one arm, a pair of aviator sunglasses held in his hand. After months of working with 14 and 15 year old boys, I realized there was a lot that could happen to a young man in about eight years. He was taller than Everett, had broader shoulders than Jude, and since I was staring, beautiful blue eyes. If he was an actual student at Parktown, I would eat my drum major whistle. Trying my best to recover, I forced myself to look away and asked hesitantly, "And you would be?"

He extended his hand for me to shake and answered, "North. Well, Ned, actually, but I usually go by my nickname. And you are?"

This was Ned?! I was supposed to take direction from the hottest guy on the planet?! For an entire season? At the moment, I couldn't even remember my own name, let alone how to conduct, or even walk.

I finally managed to mumble, "Rigby."

"That would make you the drum major?"

"Y-yes."

"Are you sure about that?" The corners of his mouth turned up. For someone who had just had a super intense conversation, he certainly recovered quickly. I didn't want to let him know I had heard part of his phone call, but at the same time, I was dying to know what all the drama was about. It then occurred to me what a killer wonderful first impression I was off to here. Thus far, I was speaking in one word answers, had turned into a 12 year old girl, and an eavesdropper, all while he was all suave and flirty. I tried to recover and answered confidently, "Yes. I'm the Parktown drum major."

Only my response came out all snotty and conceited, like I was the best drum major in the world or something. What as wrong with me?

Ned, rather North, looked strangely at me before he replied, "I'm looking forward to working with you."

Rather than return his nice comment like any normal person would do, I blurted out, "So, we need to talk."

"Yeah?"

I barged ahead. Talking to insanely hot young men was not something I exactly excelled at, or had any real practice in, so I forced myself to pretend like he was just another guy. I didn't like to start out with negatives, but I wanted this guy to know what he was getting into. I continued, "So, we had pre-Band camp this week and things didn't go as well I would've liked them to."

"I'm sure they went better than you thought they did."

"No, they didn't," I said flatly, then instantly regretted my statement. So far, I was coming off as an unconfident smart mouthed immature high school student and all in record time! What was wrong with me?

North tapped a finger on his motorcycle helmet, but said nicely, "I think I can be the judge of that."

Fortunately, Ms. Jenkins chose that moment to come in and relieve me of my extreme awkwardness.

"Hey you two! Glad to see you found each other."

I actually had to hold back a sigh, because up until about five minutes ago, I didn't realize I had been looking for anyone.

"Yes, Rigby was just telling me how pre-band camp went."

I was glad Ms. Jenkins liked to talk, because I resolved to keep my mouth shut before I did any further reputation damage. I zoned out while Ms. J went on and on (and on) about the show and our progress throughout the week. I had never once considered Ned would be someone I would be attracted to. In my mind, he had always been this dorky dude who would be nice enough and helpful, but more like a band parent than someone I would ever consider dating. In my consideration, he was never some hot guy who drove a motorcycle and had some sort of mysterious past.

"So, Rigby, can you show Ned around the school while I get those tapes?"

"Uh...sure." What else was I supposed to say?

Ms. Jenkins went into her office and I said lamely, "This is the band room."

I went to move to go on, because hey, a band room is a band room and they basically all look and smell the same.

"I see that." North paused for a moment, and stood in one place near the center of the room. He tapped his index finger on mouth and commented, "Looks like something's missing."

I looked around the room and saw what every band room has – music stands, uncomfortable chairs, percussion equipment, a banner or two, a lost and found box, old bulletins on the walls. I didn't see anything missing. I had been in this room every day for almost four years, and nothing seemed out of place.

I struggled to make direct eye contact again and asked, "What's that?"

"Trophies. Plaques. Awards."

Until that moment, our complete lack of physical recognition hadn't ever dawned on me. I thought of our competitors – were there band rooms littered with prizes and mementos from their fantastic shows? Did they have more than just pictures of previous years on their walls? I scuffed my Nike on the familiar carpet and said, "Oh yeah...we are kind of lacking in that department."

"I promise you, Rigby, at the end of the season, we'll change that."

The way he said it, I could actually believe the potential was a possibility. Still unsure how to talk to North, I joked sadly, "Maybe you should wait until you see the band before you say that..."

I walked towards the percussion room, motioning him to follow me. I didn't make it three steps before I heard him say, "Stop right there."

There was something very commanding in his voice. I stopped and turned around.

North continued, "When Ms. Jenkins talks to me about the band, she always brags about how much spirit and energy you have. She's basically told me that you, on your own, have turned this band around. Now, when I get here, I'm not sure if I caught you at a bad time, but you seem disconnected, distracted, and a bit apathetic. I don't know what you expected from me, but I don't want to hear your excuses, nor do I want to hear you putting down your band. If you are going to help lead everyone on this year, they are going to need you to be drum major 24 hours a day, 7 days a week. Do you think you can handle that?"

My mouth literally fell open. Throughout the summer, my confidence and ego had improved, only to have our pre-band camp knock it down a few pegs. Unfortunately, everything he said was true, but just because technically he was correct didn't give him the right to use the tone he had. Being in high school, I hated being the subject of snap judgments. Just because I was a teenager did not being I could automatically be lectured at or talked down to. I growled back at him, "Don't ever question me again. Maybe you are catching me on a bad day, I don't know, but you want commitment? Fine. You've got it."

"Good."

"Good. You seem like a smart guy, I'm sure you can figure out where everything else is. I'll see you this afternoon."

I turned on my heel and marched out of the room. Who did this guy think he was? How would that kind of attitude help anyone? I grumbled all the way to my car – frustrated with our introduction. At home, I found Jude at his desk, multiple textbooks spread out in front of him. Although grades came easily to him, my brother liked learning. While I had to force myself to study, he enjoyed being smart on a whole bunch of subjects. Strange, I know.

Not knowing where to start, I sat on his bed and started messing one of his many Lego sets. I knew this irritated him, so he would start talking to me.

"What do you want, Rigby?"

Launching myself from the bed, I answered, "Remember how I told you about the new instructor we were getting?"

"Yes – Nedward? What was his name?"

"It's actually North."

"Sounds dreamy." When I didn't immediately respond, Jude knew something was up and he pounced, "He is dreamy! You like him!"

I crossed my arms and said, "I most certainly do not. He's a brat. I'm not sure how I'm going to make it through band camp, let alone an entire season with him."

"Keep telling yourself that, sis."

"I've come to you for help, but I can see you're not in a particularly helpful mood."

Jude put up his hands and said, "Hold up a minute. What sort of help do you want?"

It was a good question. I actually had no idea what I wanted. Part of me wanted to redo the entire conversation I'd had with North, while the other just wanted to ignore him and get on with things. Of course, another part of me wanted to kiss him senseless – and I wasn't particularly ready to deal with those emotions. I hadn't liked a guy since Everett and my libido decides to come back with some off limits jerkstore? Thanks a lot, hormones. Whatever feelings I was having, I certainly didn't want my brother involved, so I moved towards the door and said, "None for now."

Jude looked at me and said, "I don't believe you, but good luck with everything."

"Thanks, bro."

I managed to calm down and collect myself before rejoining the band after lunch. I hadn't given Ms. Jenkins a reason for my sudden departure, but she didn't question my absence and I decided to keep things moving forward. I hoped North hadn't decided to rat me out for being immature to my band director. Approaching the band room, I noticed the energy was practically electric. I smiled as I walked through the sections, happy that everyone seemed ready to show off for our new instructor. Even though we were having band camp at the school, the hours were longer, the commitment bigger and I think I had managed to instill in everyone how important our efforts were and that we were on the edge of taking our program to the next level. Things might also have been upped because this was the last week before school began. Nearing the band director's office, I noticed North and Ms. Jenkins talking to each other behind the closed door. This was good, because I wasn't sure what I wanted to say to Mr. Ned 'North' Buchanan. I had sorted through my feelings, and had to admit that no matter what my first impression had been, our new instructor had the right attitude for the band. Not ready to face him, I avoided the pair, wondering when they were going to get started. Finally, I saw the door open, and North walked to the front of the band room, nodding at me on the way. Innately, I understood what he was asking and clapped my hands for attention. The band, I think sensed something different, something that said, 'this is important guys – pay attention and snapped to ready positions.' I nodded back at North.

From the director's stand, he spoke confidently, "Alright Parktown. My name is North Buchanan and I'm really looking forward to working with all of you this season. I know you've been practicing hard all summer and I can't wait to see what you've got for me. You should know I have some serious goals for us this fall and I hope we all look back in a few months and are very proud of our accomplishments. For today, I'd like you to break into sectionals as scheduled this morning. I'll be checking in on all of you, to see where we are and figure out how we can make things better. This afternoon, we're going to start with the drill for the show."

As much as I didn't want to admit it, North's voice did inspire patience. The sections dismissed and walked their separate ways and usual places to practice. I walked up to North and asked politely, "What do you want me to do?"

"What do you usually do?"

"Go to each section and help them work through their parts. I've already memorized the score." I had spent a solid week constantly listening to the show on mp3 and felt comfortable with my progress. I still needed work adding cues, but I was on pace for where I wanted to be.

"Any problem sections I should know about?"

"The color guard. The drumline," I answered without hesitation.

North's lips pursed for a moment before he answered, "Who do you least want to talk to?"

Was this some sort of weird test? I said, "The drumline."

"So, I'll look into the color guard..."

"Wait, what?" I interrupted. Didn't he hear what I had said?

"Rigby, consider this your first lesson. You need to take on what is most difficult. Consider it a challenge."

I wanted to grumble, to complain, but deep down, I knew he was right.

He asked, "Is there something I should know? Some reason you don't want to bother with them? Weren't they your former section?"

"Nothing that has any relevance now," I answered, not wanting to go into the tragic back story that was me and Everett.

"Then go talk to the drumline."

"Fine."

"I'll see you in two hours and we'll talk about what progress you made."

Chapter 6: Growing Pains

I silently cursed North on my long walk around the school to find my old section. I didn't like being bossed around, because, well, that was my job – and one I had been more or less perfecting all summer. Still mumbling to the empty lockers, I guess I had either consciously ignored the fact "Ned" was going to come in and actually have control over the band, or I thought he and I would be more of a partnership and less of a dictatorship. Taking a deep breath and forcing myself not to whip out my phone and text Jude and complain about stuff he had no chance of understanding, until proven otherwise, I needed to respect North and whatever his method was going to be of making our band the best.

As I approached the drummers, I realized I really should've addressed them sometime last week. They weren't even pretending to practice. The percussionists were in various degrees of doing nothing – from braiding each other's hair to simply banging around on their instruments. As I was already wound up from my interaction with North, it took me about two seconds to get seriously livid. Sure, I was partially mad at myself for letting things go on this long, but mostly mad at Everett for not living up to his end of the bargain. Probably, the fictional "Being a Swell Drum Major" textbook would tell me to pull my ex-boyfriend aside and talk to him away from everyone else, but I was more than ready to throw the textbook out and get some work done. For reasons I didn't want to address, as much as North had pissed me off, I wanted to rise to the challenge and show him how much I could accomplish in a session.

Taking a deep breath, I blew my whistle, loudly.

Everyone immediately looked up.

"What in the hell are you guys doing?" I asked, hands on my hips.

No one answered.

"Can anyone tell me what they are supposed to be doing right now?" I tried to keep the rage out of my voice.

Everett answered sarcastically, "Working on our screenplay?"

The rest of the drumline laughed and giggled nervously. Their captain was referencing a long and involved inside joke from the previous season, but this was not the time for laughing or joking. However, my section hadn't given up on me entirely – I could tell they were waiting for my reaction. As a group, we were definitely in unchartered territory. For as long as anyone had known Everett and I, they had known 'us' together – happy, in love, in harmony, all that stuff. To put it plainly, they had never seen Mom and Dad fight before.

Trying to remind myself that North or Ms. Jenkins could come around the corner at any minute, I resisted the urge to curse hysterically. I counted to three, and answered calmly, "No, Everett, as much as we would all like to see a sequel to 'The Cat Parade' that is not what you are supposed to be doing. Can anyone else tell me what the rest of the band is doing?"

Ashley, a sophomore and one of our three cymbal players, raised her hand and asked hesitantly, "Practicing?"

I nodded and said, "Exactly. So, why are none of you practicing? Have you already memorized the part? Are you that far ahead? Because if you are, I'd like to hear your progress."

Their response was a group effort of looking down and mumbling. No one risked making eye contact with me.

I crossed my arms and continued, "That's what I thought. Get your instruments on their stands, get your music out and set up, because as of now, I'm running this rehearsal."

I was pulling rank over Everett, a first for the Parktown Pirates marching band. Generally, each section leader had nearly complete authority over their section. I would make suggestions, but trusted the leadership to run things their own way. So far this season I had never had to so literally use my role to get things done. People and sections respected me. I shot a look to Everett begging him not to challenge me. He looked away, clearly uncomfortable. The situation was not how I wanted things to be, but I wasn't going to let anyone get in the way of my dream to turn this band around. Not to mention, I had been sent over here by North and I sure as heck wasn't going to go back without accomplishing what I needed to do.

The practice was one I would rather forget. The playing was uninspired and embarrassing. While some sections were better than others, as a whole, the drumline had barely made it through the opener. No one could play at tempo, not one note had been memorized, and the lack of discipline was even worse than I remembered. They were unmotivated and Everett was radiating with anger. When the world's slowest sectional was finally over, it felt like we had been practicing for days and had nothing to show for our efforts. Maybe I was in over my head. Maybe my dream of elevating our band was an impossible one.

I barked out, "You guys had better shape up tonight when we learn drill!"

As soon as the words came out of my mouth, I realized what a terrible source of help and inspiration I was. While the group all moped back into the school, I waited for Everett's inevitable tirade. I knew he was angry, but wasn't sure what the fallout was going to be.

I decided to start things and said, "It didn't have to be like this."

"You didn't give me a chance."

"Didn't I? I've given you your space all summer to make this section into something everyone could be proud of and look where my decision got me. Whatever happened to that meeting we had in the spring? Weren't you supposed to support me?"

He was quiet a moment before he answered, "Maybe I didn't want any space..."

"What did you want?"

"It doesn't matter now, does it?"

"What's that supposed to mean?"

"I think you made it pretty obvious the other night."

"I—"

"Rigby?"

It was North and I was actually elated to see him. My feelings (and frustrations) for Everett were entirely too complicated to get into at that moment. I knew I owed my ex-boyfriend a little more than what we could get into at the end of an absolutely asstastic practice.

"Yes?" I asked a little too brightly.

"Ready to go over the drill?"

I looked back at Everett, who had already slunk off, but not before shooting an angry glance my way.

"Sounds great!"

We walked for a few moments before North, obviously not an idiot, asked, "Was I interrupting anything just then?"

Why was North always catching me at my worst? Couldn't he just once see me as the cool and collected individual I was? Seriously. Too quickly, I challenged, "No, we were just talking about the opener."

Although I'm pretty sure North didn't believe a word I said, he thankfully dropped the subject and asked, "How did rehearsal go?"

I think my body language did the talking for me. Before I realized what I was doing, my shoulders had slumped, and I was looking at the ground. By now we had walked inside the school, through the deserted band room and back to Ms. Jenkins' office. Anyone with a car had quickly split in search of fast food and a bit of rest for the dinner break. The underclassmen either hitched a ride, or went to someone's house close to the school. Rather than waste time on section that wasted my time, I had wanted to go over drill with North and Ms. Jenkins during the break. Unfortunately, Ms. Jenkins had also scheduled herself for a meeting with the band parents during that time to talk about the upcoming season. I spied some leftover pizza on my band director's desk, so I grabbed a piece and finally replied, "I've had better. How was yours?"

North quirked an eyebrow and answered, "I can see what you mean about the color guard, they definitely need work, but let's start with you, what exactly did you accomplish?"

Besides completely alienating the drumline captain? I avoided eye contact and replied honestly, "I think we made it through the Opener once. However, they might need some extra work with the parts. We've never played anything like you've written before."

North leaned over and admitted, "I'll let you in on a little secret."

"What's that?" I asked warily.

"I didn't write that part – a friend of mine helped me."

Was this his way of getting to know me? By confiding a weird thing with me? Was this guy socially backwards? I couldn't understand what he was trying to tell me.

"Umm...okay. Can you still help with it?"

North smiled and said, "Come on Rigby, I'm just trying to get you to loosen up a little bit. Do I need to remind you this is just high school?"

I gritted my teeth, because, yes, while this was high school, to me it was a lot more. Not sure what sort of response I should give, I said, "I'll try. So, how about you? How did work out with the girls? Did you make any progress?"

"I should tell you that I've recommended to Ms. J that we bring in additional help for their section. I'm good at a lot of things, but color guard is certainly not one of them."

I decided this information was very good news. At least North could admit his mistakes or when he was in over his head, plus, I had to give him props for acting so quickly. Maybe I had been too quick to judge our instructor. After all, he was being nice to me, doing his best to help the band, and, at the end of the day, who wouldn't want an older attractive man in their life?

Somehow, the obvious attempts North was making to get me to chill out and move on made him even more attractive. I asked, "Do you think she'll go for it?"

"I don't know. It could be difficult trying to find someone this late in the pre-season, but maybe she can ask around."

I thought a moment before I casually questioned, "Do you know anyone?"

He looked away for a long moment, as if he was deciding the most appropriate answer, and said uncomfortably, "Not really."

And, it could've been my imagination, but it sounded like he was changing the subject, when he continued, "So, here's how I thought we would break down the opener."

The evening practice went infinitely better than the afternoon one. The opener (the first song in our trip around the world) started with God Save the Queen and went into a quick Beatles medley and already had more sets than our previous show did combined. I was happy to see all of the members of the band staying at attention and not getting frustrated as we reset over and over again. The last couple of times, we even added the music. Now, the effort wasn't anything spectacular, and there was plenty of phasing, but somehow we managed to all finish the song together and there were smiles on everyone's faces as we finished.

From my perch on the podium, I announced, "Great job today band, and, as promised, I'd like to announce the first ever section of the day. Congratulations to the saxophone section!"

Predictably, the saxes went crazy – high fiving and strutting around from their spot near the 40 yard line. I was delighted to see other sections look on jealously. Over the summer I had begged from various local restaurants a variety of 'free stuff' coupons to give away to the section that showed the overall best band spirit and commitment for the day. Today's gift was for some very delicious gourmet ice cream.

I added, "We'll see everyone for practice tomorrow morning! Don't forget your sunscreen and water! Get some rest tonight."

The band broke and went on their way. I was sure the other seniors and upperclassmen would be gathering somewhere, but after today's events, I could admit I was completely worn out and only interested in a shower and my bed.

Driving to practice the next morning, I was cautiously optimistic and also a bit melancholy. Summer was officially coming to an end. School was going to start soon and part of me wished I could continue in a pattern of practicing and not having to worry about anything else. While I knew Jude was excited to get his senior year done and over with – to move on to bigger and better things than Parktown, I happened to finally like where I was. I was comfortable as drum major. The introduction of North made life interesting and if I had some sort of cosmic remote, I would put it on pause and stay in this week of band camp. Inside the school, as we gathered for practice, Ms. Jenkins motioned for North and me to join her in her office. Closing the door, she said, "Well, North, I followed your advice about the color guard."

North and I looked and shared a quick smile with each other – this was great news.

I asked, "That's excellent – what's her story?"

Ms. Jenkins replied in an excited tone, "Her name is Denise D'Amato. She comes highly recommended. In fact, North, she seemed to know exactly who you were and was really looking forward to working with you."

I looked over to see North's reaction, and was genuinely surprised to see the blood draining from his face. While Ms. Jenkins continued talking about the additional help, I wondered what would cause such a response in him.

Chapter 7: Two Steps Forward

Ms. Jenkins, apparently oblivious to North's paling beneath his tan, stood up and said, "Alright gang, let's get started on our second day! Rigby, why don't you tell the color guard the good news this morning?"

I nodded enthusiastically, while North slunk out of the room ahead of me. I wanted to ask him what the heck was going on, but there was no privacy in the crowded band room. Without thinking, I reached out to tug on his shirt. North snapped out of whatever funk he was in and asked, "What?"

"Are you okay?"

"I... I'm not sure yet."

Granted I had known North for all of 24 hours, but I was genuinely concerned for him. I asked, "Is it something I can help with?"

"No, I just..." Something seemed to switch in him and he said, "So, after you tell the guard, why don't you stay with them? I'll look after the drumline."

In no hurry to get into things with Everett, I flashed him a thumbs up, but resolved to find out more about what was going on with our potential color guard instructor and North.

After calling the band to attention and dismissing them for sectionals, I realized I had to hand things to North, he was handling whatever his inner issues were like a professional. It took me a moment to put myself in his Vans and realize he was on his own in a new town, with a giant responsibility – not exactly the easiest choice one could make. Even from just a day of interacting with the band, I could tell any number of programs would be lucky to have him. What was it about us? One day over the summer when Ms. Jenkins was on the phone, I had looked at our meager budget and knew North wasn't at Parktown for the money. Of course, this wasn't the kind of answer you could demand out of someone after knowing them for about a day, so I guess I would have to wait and see.

After checking in on the wind players, my rehearsal with the ladies and gentleman of the color guard did not get off to a very good start. Although Adelaide was a very talented twirler, she didn't seem too concerned with putting together an actual routine, or sharing her skills with the rest of the group. I hoped this Denise chick could get here sooner rather than later. The thing about marching band I was realizing is, you could have the best trumpet section in the world, but if the rest of the band was only mediocre then it's not like you could to clean up at awards time. Even after all the progress I thought we had made, the Color guard was so disorganized, I didn't even know where to start and, unless you considered dragging the flags on the ground in unison, I was definitely not a choreographer. I had a mental debate about forcing some punishment on the section, but decided any reprimand I gave them would probably not reach its desired effect. Discipline was not something they understood or respected.

"What did you do with North yesterday?" I asked, then immediately wished I hadn't. Apparently, my question opened the door for an unmitigated response of barely contained North crushes to be released.

I held up my hands, and, over the comments, said, "Okay, besides falling in love with our Instructor, did he give you girls anything to work on?"

In a similar move the drumline gave me the day before, the girls all kind of looked around at each other before Adelaide replied, "Oh! Yes, he gave us kind of a basic idea for the opener."

One of the underclassmen asked, "So, we're supposed to run around those sets and twirl at the same time?"

With as much patience as I could muster, I sighed and said, "I know in previous seasons we've done a lot of standing around and twirling, but have you ever noticed what the best bands do?"

Fortunately, it only took the sophomore a moment to answer, "Oh...."

I nodded and said, "So that's what we want to do, and for that I have some great news."

The section looked at each other warily, before I announced, "Ms. Jenkins has secured a color guard instructor for the season! She'll be here soon!"

The girls looked around at each other, unsure how to take the news. Of all the sections in the band, this one was still the one I worried about the most. While everyone else had come together with their footwork and musicality, the color guard was still severely lacking. They were the most visible part of the band, and clearly had the furthest to go. I had struggled over the summer with what exactly to do with the situation, which ultimately, I had no control over. Short of cutting them altogether (which in all honestly, just seemed like giving up), there wasn't much I could do. Sure, I might be able to get them in step, but I didn't know the first thing about what color guard judges would be looking for. Overall, general effect counted for something and I wasn't going to write those points off just yet. I had voiced my concerns on multiple occasions to Ms. Jenkins, who had assured me everything would work out.

However depressed thinking about the color guard made me, it made me also realize I still had hope in the drumline. I knew its members, knew what they were capable of, and hoped they would ultimately come through. The part they had been given was just too cool not to figure out – whoever wrote it was a creative percussionist who didn't cut corners or sacrifice anything. If our Line could pull off this book, there was a chance they even might be able to win something out of it.

I finished, "So, let's spend this week getting ready for her. Don't you want Denise to be impressed when she gets here?"

It seemed they actually did. While I clapped, and counted over and over again, the girls got closer to a unison performance.

Tired and sweaty, I met up with Ms. Jenkins and North after the end of the drill rehearsal that day. We had one of best practices yet, and made real progress going into the second song – some sort of Russian folk dance. The melody was catchy in a weird way, and I think the baritones had already come up with some inappropriate lyrics for the tune. I'm not sure what North said to the Line, but they sounded about a million times better than the day before. Their progress was on my growing list of things to follow up with North.

Ms. Jenkins was seated at her desk, checking something on her computer. Clicking a few things, she turned to us with a smile, and said, "I just got an e-mail from Denise – looks like she'll be here next week."

"Is she here for the whole season?" In my excitement earlier, I forgot to ask.

"At the moment, I've contracted her for six weeks, and then we'll see what we can do with the budget."

I looked over to North for his response, but he seemed to be doing the same thing as earlier – that is, remaining completely silent.

We talked for a few more minutes about how things were going with the week and what we were going to work on for tomorrow, and then it was time to leave. North collected his motorcycle helmet and I grabbed my bag, intent on following him to ask him what was going on. As soon as we had cleared the band room, I asked, "So, what gives with you and this Denise chick?"

For a moment, I wondered if I stepped way over the line. Then, I saw the half-smile returned to his face. He sighed and answered, "Rigby?"

"Yes?'

"Has anyone told you that you're too perceptive for a high school student?"

I guess I should have been offended, however, I laughed and answered, "Seriously, no. Jude is the one who inherited all those genes."

"Who's Jude?"

"My twin brother. I haven't mentioned him yet?" I realized, of course I hadn't because, up to this point, I hadn't had a truly normal conversation with North. In a way, him not knowing about Jude was kind of nice, because having been a twin and growing in Parktown, the twin status was usually how people defined us. North was probably one of the first people who knew me as 'Rigby,' and not 'Rigby – Jude's twin sister.'

North shrugged and answered, "No, but, cool. So, who's technically older?"

I boasted, "I am, but don't think we're going to start talking about my family all of the sudden and forget about what I asked you in the first place. You're North Buchanan, why are you worried about some color guard instructor?"

He was quiet for a long time, before he finally replied, "I don't want to get into it."

"Fine. So, how did you get the Line to come around today?" I asked, wondering if there was some big secret.

"I appealed to their egos. I listed off how great the other sections were doing and if they stepped things up, their contribution would give us a real chance at competitions. I think they didn't want to be the section holding the band back."

"Whatever it takes."

"Everett's a pretty good captain."

"I guess."

"Sounds like there's more to the story."

"I don't want to get into it," I quoted North's words back to him.

"Have a good night, Rigby."

"You too, North."

By the end of the week, the Parktown marching band was sore, tired, sunburned, but have somehow managed to get through the first three songs and even tackled the difficult closer. We had mostly memorized the drill to the first two movements and the color guard seemed to be dropping less. Ms. Jenkins even arranged a 'performance' after the last rehearsal for all the parents, siblings (yay Jude!), friends, relatives, etc. Given the heat, it was too hot for uniforms, so everyone was wearing khaki shorts and our newly acquired band shirts (designed by the lovely Heather) to show some uniformity. As Everett tapped out quarter notes and the band marched to opening set, Ms. Jenkins listed the section leaders over the speaker.

I clapped and brought the band to a parade rest, then waited for my question.

"Drum major, is your band ready to take the field for competition?" North's voice called out.

Alone, with the breeze gently blowing my hair, I clapped, called the band to attention, snapped off my smart salute, marched to the podium, quickly climbed up, then blew the whistle and held my hands for attention. Even though I was wearing my sunglasses, I looked around the field for a few moments and checked to see the opening set was as it should be.

"Dress center, dress!"

Adjustments were made across the field and the opening set pulled to a sharper focus. Satisfied, I clapped my hands and shouted, "Mark time, mark."

I knew we were being videotaped – something North and I had worked out was going to be reviewing our filmed performances at least once a week with the band, so I stood up extra straight and let the show take me away. As I expected, there was phasing, and the color guard kind of looked out of place for a majority of the ballad, but, overall, we were in a good starting place and miles beyond where we usually were for this time of year.

Wiping the sweat from my eyes, I brought my hands down at the end of the closer, a big smile on my face.

After congratulations all around from our parents and family (including a relatively rushed introduction of my parents and brother to North), we all eventually made it back to the band room and, after storing our instruments, the marching Pirates quickly dispersed. I couldn't blame them – school was about to start and everyone was interested in making the best use of their remaining minutes of summer. Without a section, I found my friend group significantly reduced, but that fact didn't bother me. Over the summer, Heather had taken an interest in the male clarinet transfer from another school and I wanted to give them some space. Trying to commit my week to memory, I packed up my stuff slowly – hesitant to leave. Without much effort, North came instantly to my head. During the week, I had a lot of time to not only interact with our instructor, but also to observe him. He had a crazy reserve of patience I could only dream about – he handled the obvious crushes with class and tact. He spoke to the guys in the band with respect and made the rookies feel like they were an integral part of the band. As far as I had brought us with my efforts, there was just something about him everyone responded positively to. I had tried to deny my own growing crush, but finally just gave up and came to the conclusion that if I wasn't going to date anyone this season, at least some unrequited love would help me get through things. At the same time, to open another chapter, I needed to officially close the book on my past.

"Hey, Ev…"

I had been lurking, trying to time out things perfectly. The Line had pretty much cleared the percussion room, giving us some privacy.

"Yes?" He turned around, and seeing who I was, responded in a disappointed tone, "What do you want?"

"I wanted to tell you, good job today, and this week. The section is really improving." I resisted the urge to add the improvement was probably mostly as a result of daily interaction with North, and not so much Everett's leadership.

"Thanks."

"Do you have a minute?"

He looked around the room and finally said, "I guess we're getting there."

I wanted to get him on a neutral playing field and the percussion room was definitely not that place. Neither was the band room. And actually the school was probably out of the question as well – having been together for so long, we had memories almost everywhere.

"Walk me to my car?" I asked, knowing he was a gentleman and wouldn't refuse my offer.

"Sure."

I had debated with myself how to start this conversation for a long time. I didn't want to apologize for what I had done, because really, I didn't think I had anything to be sorry for. We walked in silence, past the montage that had been our relationship – the halls where we had held hands, the locker where he had asked me to Prom, the classrooms he had walked me to. Once outside, I took a deep breath and asked, "So, what did you mean earlier? About this summer? And space?"

"I don't know, Rigby, nothing's working out the way I thought it was going to this year."

"And that's my fault?"

"Yes...no...I don't know."

Arriving at our cars, I said, "I'm disappointed in you, Ev."

"I can say the same for you."

I tried to keep my voice even as I responded, "Touché." Looking away, I added, "Look, I just need to know whatever we have personally going on off the field, it won't effect what happens on the field."

"I don't know if I can make that promise."

Frustrated, I blurted out, "Then what is it going to take? You've had all summer!"

"Did you ever think maybe it would take longer for me to get over you than the five seconds it took for you to get over me?!"

Up until that moment, I hadn't actually considered that fact.

He continued, "You didn't, did you? So, while it's all well and good for you to tell me to keep things all non-personal between us, you'll have to excuse me for still trying to sort things out. I'm not some sort of robot. What did I do, Riggs? Why don't you want to be with me?"

"I don't know what to say..."

"You've already said enough. Just stay away from me. It seems to be the only thing that works between us. Don't worry, you don't need to bother yourself with the drumline any more. We'll be fine, just don't get involved."

Watching Everett walk away, all the highs I had felt from the performance earlier that day came crashing down. Sure, I might be on my way to having an award-winning band, but what had I sacrificed to make that happen? I had basically stepped all over one of the most important people in the world to me and had no idea how to make it right.

I headed home, in need of talking to the most important person in my life – Jude.

Chapter 8: Enter Denise

"Hey Jude?"

My brother was rummaging around in the kitchen, most likely looking for something to eat. In preparation for the upcoming cross-country season, his metabolism was going crazy.

"Yo," came his voice from inside the pantry and, breakfast pastry in hand, he said, "Score, Pop Tarts!"

I could tell we were about to have an outstanding heart to heart.

"Put one in for me, will you?" I asked.

What? Conducting makes a girl hungry. Thirty seconds later we were holding our piping hot treats when Jude commented, "By the way, great show today."

"Aww, you're just saying that because you're related to the drum major."

"No, I mean it. I don't know a lot about band, but things looked and sounded a lot better this time."

"Well, thanks." No matter how good I thought the show was personally; it still felt good to hear someone reinforce my feelings.

"So, what else have you been up to this week? I feel like we haven't talked since you got all out of whack with the instructor."

"Oh, you know…"

"No, I don't, that's why I'm asking."

I looked to see if our parents were around – they weren't – and continued dramatically, "I think I finally ended things with Everett."

"Really?"

"Yup." I didn't usually discuss my love life with Jude, but somehow, on this particular subject, I wanted his opinion.

"Well, that's good. I mean, it took you long enough, but I'm glad."

I considered his response before I said, "Why's that? Didn't you like Ev?"

"Don't get me wrong, I did like him. I still like thing he's an okay guy." And I knew Jude wasn't lying, because every once in awhile during Ev and I's three year relationship, if my brother was actually dating a girl for longer than two weeks, the four of us would go out together on a double date and the guys would more or less get along and have a good time.

"But?"

"I didn't want you to be one of those girls who dated the same guy all through high school. You're just to cool for that."

"Were you ever planning on sharing this little fact with me?"

Jude took a big bite of Pop Tart, chewed and swallowed before he responded, "I guess if you two did something crazy like get engaged, eventually, but hey, I didn't have to because you worked it out yourself."

"I just feel kind of guilty. Is that normal?"

Jude rolled his eyes, and answered, "Why?"

"Everett's kind of blaming me for the fact that his senior year sucks."

"First of all, our senior year hasn't even officially started. Second of all, isn't that a lot of pressure to put on you, all because you broke up with him? What is he, a girl?"

"No, Mr. Sensitivity, but maybe he's right."

"Look, Rig, if you were with him, then you'd be the unhappy one with the sucky senior year."

However crass Jude's response sounded, my brother was right. I couldn't carry around a bunch of guilt because Everett had chosen to mope around about me. I hadn't cheated on him or anything despicable like that. It had been a clean break.

"Anyway, since you guys have technically been broken since like, April or whatever, please tell me you have someone else in mind? You let the whole summer go by and I didn't say anything, but this has gone on long enough."

Instead of answering, I blushed and finished off my pop tart.

Eyebrows raised, Jude asked, "So there is someone? Do I know him?"

I didn't want to answer this question, because I knew as soon as I actually said the words out loud that I liked North, there would be no taking it back. The crush would be official.

"It's the band instructor," I blurted out, desperately needing to share my feelings with someone.

Jude was quiet a moment before he asked, "And you're sure it's not some sort of weird rebound thing? Some sort of unattainable guy because it's safe to like someone you can't have?"

I thought a moment – were my feelings just some sort of weird emotional attachment to North specifically? Or to someone in general? Everyone needed a different amount of time between relationships, had North come along at exactly the right time? Or was I just in need of liking someone again? And was North that unattainable?

Just because he was our instructor, did that mean we could never be together? Was it the same thing as having a crush on one of the One Direction lads? In response, I gave a non-committal shrug.

My brother continued, "And why am I bothering to ask that anyway, isn't he off limits?"

I sighed deeply and answered, "He is."

"So maybe, rather than develop real feelings for someone, you decided to like the one guy you couldn't be with, even if he did like you back?"

"Why do you have to always make everything so complicated?"

Rather than get angry with me, Jude said, "Don't blame me for what you are personally choosing to do. I don't see why you don't do what I do, anyway."

Jude chose to keep his love life like Joey from Friends or Barney from How I Met Your Mother. Sometimes, his behavior made me wonder if we were really twins. Unfortunately, our parents had the pictures to prove our identities.

"There are double standards, Jude, and you know that. If I went through guys like you go through girls, well...that's not the reputation I'm after. Also, unlike you – I happen to like monogamy."

"That may be true, but whatever, before you decide to invest to some real feelings in this North fellow, why don't you think about it first?"

"Thanks, bro, I will."

Even though I knew my brother was the king of the short term relationship, there was still some truth to his advice.

No closer to sorting through my feelings for North, my last first day of school arrived without much fanfare. To be honest, I had been looking forward to finishing the halftime show than I was about some random Monday in August. After going through the usual first day motions, I made my way out to the parking lot to wait for Denise, ready to greet her and welcome her into the Parktown family. Unsure about her past or complications with North, I had mixed feelings about her arrival. More than anything, I knew we desperately needed the help, but I wasn't sure what additional drama she might bring. I tried to remind myself that my big dreams of a cohesive marching band were close to becoming a reality and furthermore, whatever relationship Denise and North had, ultimately, it was none of my business. I didn't have to wait long and glimpsed Denise before she found me. I mean, this girl had to be Denise, because she certainly wasn't a student at Parktown. If she was, my brother definitely would have dated her. Denise was blonde, fit, and perfect. As she struggled to get her equipment out of the car, I walked up to help her. Even though I had a bad start with North, that didn't mean I had to do the same with our other instructor.

"Here, need a hand?" I made a grab for a pair of rifles.

She squinted at me and said, "Sure, thanks."

"By the way, I'm Rigby."

There was a blank stare.

I cleared my throat and clarified, "Umm…the drum major?"

Another quizzical look.

"Aren't you here to help out with the Parktown marching band? Sorry, I saw your equipment and thought…" I trailed off on purpose, hoping she would say something affirmative to stop my babbling.

"Yes, well, that's one of the reasons I'm here," she answered in a distracted tone, as she sorted through the trunk of her car.

I tried to think of all the other reasons she could be instructing a less than mediocre color guard in a nowhere town, and came up short. I decided to give a vague noncommittal answer, "That's interesting."

Plucking out a duffle bag and closing the trunk door with a slam, she stated simply, "Yeah, I'm going to help out or whatever, but one of the big reasons I'm here is to convince North that he was wrong about me."

A record scratch sounded in my head.

"As in the band instructor?" I clarified, hoping there might be a mystery North somewhere out there I didn't know about, or somehow, if she meant our North, that maybe, she was going to convince him of something not in the realm of romance.

"That would be him," she replied with a smug smile on her face I instantly hated.

Aside from the obvious inappropriateness of this conversation, something struck me as very odd at this point. North, thus far, or at least to me, had been very introverted, and not exactly forthcoming in the mystery that was his life pre-Parktown. Sure, we had talked endlessly about the show, and had even developed an inside joke or two about the process, but I was having a difficult time getting to know who North the guy was, and here was a girl who obviously had some insight into his life. I was left with no choice. If Denise had somehow come to the decision she was going to volunteer intimate details about her life, then who was I to argue?

"What happened exactly to make him think otherwise?" I questioned. Sure, we probably should've been talking about the opening sets and how better to showcase the color guard in the closer, but I had to know.

"We used to date."

Even though that statement made my heart drop into my stomach and confirmed what I had already guessed, it wasn't difficult to picture the two of them together. In an instant, Denise's confession also totally solidified my crush as exactly that – a crush. If North was going around dating hot color guard instructors, then he was never going to realistically look at me as someone he could potentially call his girlfriend. That fact somehow made me very sad. And that fact made me worried. Jude had told me to examine my feelings for North before I committed to the crush, and judging by my quick reaction to Denise, well, it didn't feel like a rebound kind of reaction – my nascent feelings felt like something much more. Furthermore, and even more depressing, Denise's revelations threw up another barrier in the way between me and a normal, competition-winning, season. How was I supposed to act normally around her when her very existence was irritating me? I was immature yes, but could nothing go right?

As I debated what to say next, I figured North wasn't exactly going to sit down and tell me this particular story any time soon, so I asked, "How long ago?"

"Just a few months ago – he broke things off around the end of April."

As we walked, I asked, "How long were you together?" somehow hoping my question came off more like, 'we're-bonding-as-girls' and not 'I-totally-want-to-date-your-ex-boyfriend-and-am-trying-to-get-information-out-of-you.'

"I don't know, off and on for at least two years," she answered in a distracted tone.

Yikes, not really the answer I wanted to hear. Still, if her response was any consolation, I was pretty sure I had distinctly overheard North telling her to stay away – and he sounded pretty serious about it.

"What exactly happened?" I asked, still desperate for details.

As we were almost inside the school, Denise finally seemed to realize this was a weird conversation to be having with a complete stranger and paused for a moment. Of course, whatever policy she had on sharing very personal information with new people didn't stop her from giving this completely unexpected response, "I cheated on him."

Well, if I ever needed another reason to completely dislike her, now I had all the ammunition I required. Knowing this fact was like another part of the North puzzle fitting into place. Of course, the conversation made the Denise mystery that much larger and, quite honestly, it took some points away from both teams – North for dating her for so long (seriously!), Denise for being a cheater and coming to North when he so clearly didn't want her there.

I called on all my acting skills and replied, "I'm sure you had a reason."

"That's the thing – I totally did! Everyone was all 'I can't believe you'd make out with Owen – he's North's best friend,' but I promise it made sense at the time."

Like trying to come up with alternative reasons for Denise to be in Parktown, I tried envision reasons to make out with someone's best friend, let alone cheat on the lovable North, but came up empty.

"It was all a test, obviously."

I was glad we were in the band room by now, because I literally could not think of something to say in response. In a matter of minutes, I had been roped into more drama than my previous three years combined. I mean, was I that naïve? Even Jude, with his constant dating, at least clearly ended one relationship before starting another and never poached another dude's girl.

"Here's the band room," I said awkwardly, knowing North was probably somewhere close by and due to my usual amazing timing, he was most likely going to walk in on his ex-girlfriend and I's getting to know you chat – therefore completely eliminating any possibility of seeing me as a friend ever again.

"...so, I'm just going to check in with some sections – see you later."

I practically ran out of the room, unprepared with what the past few minutes had dealt me. Unlike North, who was legitimately interested in helping fix our band, I got the feeling Denise's main reason for being here was for reuniting with North first and the color guard as an afterthought.

What was I going to do?

What if Denise sucked all of North's concentration away from the band?

I couldn't talk to North about her, could I? It felt like I had already gone behind his back a bit with all the information I know knew about him. If the tables were turned, I wouldn't want North getting all chatty with Everett. Whatever North learned about my past, I wanted to come from me and not some outside source. As optimistic as I had initially been, my senior year wasn't getting off to a very promising start as I had hoped.

Chapter 9: Unexpected

For the casual observer, it seemed North was using the same strategy I was – that is, not dealing with the situation or avoiding it entirely. For the rest of the afternoon, I did not see him and Denise together, which relieved me. Although, I don't think the lack of connection wasn't from her persistence. In the span of the two hour practice, the color guard must've switched where they were practicing at least three times, probably in search of North. Of course, it did briefly occur to me that I was wasting valuable time and energy on the non-existent potential North/Denise problem rather than my own band, but I figured I had already put in more than enough work that an hour or two wasn't going to make or break the season.

"You okay?" Heather asked as she approached me during a water break.

"Yeah."

"You seem a bit distracted."

"I'm fine, just worried about all my AP classes this semester. I'm not sure what I was thinking," I lied easily, and then said, "I think Jenkins needs me in her office – talk soon?"

"Okay," Heather answered. "But let me know if you need to talk about anything."

"I will," I answered, feeling lucky I had someone on my side.

Seeing Denise and North already inside, I hurried to join the group. Ms. Jenkins, completely unaware of all the drama that was swirling around her office, said, "Hey team, I've got some great news."

Ms. J had been on a permanent case of optimism since band camp last week, so much so that literally everything (from music to lunch to her new shoelaces) was 'good,' 'great,' or 'awesome!' For the most part, her slightly overwhelming enthusiasm was okay, but sometimes, her attitude was just plain annoying.

"...I've decided we should perform at the upcoming county marching review!"

I was a bit surprised. The review was an annual pre-competition meeting for all the better bands in the county. Given how early it was in the season, the event was kind of a way for everyone to perform and have some pseudo judging. It was rare that all the bands in the county would be present at once, so the festival was something everyone usually looked forward to. We sometimes attended, but only to watch, because, let's face it, we already had enough embarrassment to look forward to later in the season. Ms. Jenkins always claimed our lack of participation was because 'our show wasn't ready to share,' (which was true), but I think we all knew otherwise.

Ms. Jenkins's announcement caught me off guard and my heart rate increased significantly. For so long, the whole competitive element of our show had always been a future and distant event. So much so, I think I even managed to forget that one day we would actually be judged for our performance. I asked, "When is it?"

"Two weeks from tomorrow."

"What?!" I exclaimed and immediately shot up out of my seat. There was still so much to do, how would we get it done in time?

North reached over, put a gentle hand on my shoulder, and said, "Rigby, it's going to be okay, and remember, it's not actually a competition. I think it sounds like a good idea. We can get some feedback from the judges."

Although my heart continued to beat faster (mainly because of the interaction with North), I started breathing normally again and asked, "Do you really think so?"

I'd like to point out that thus far, Denise might as well have not even been in the room. She hadn't added anything. If we didn't have this festival coming up, I wondered if we needed her help at all.

North stated confidently, "I think you'll be surprised. I think this will give everyone something extra to work towards. Have some faith in your band."

For the next two weeks, while the Parktown Pirates were hard at work on our Around the World in Nine Minutes show, North ignored Denise and Everett ignored me. This fact was made much better by the fact that while I couldn't say exactly, I was under the definite impression that North was flirting with me. My romance meter was quite possibly broken or perhaps it was all one sided, but I sensed a growing tension between us. I could potentially be reading into things, but there were half smiles and more physical contact than was necessary. While the developments with North secretly thrilled me, I quickly noticed however friendly Denise had been to me when she first arrived, she quickly changed her tune. I think some girls have a built in sensor when it comes to knowing when other girls (erm, me) like their guy. More often than not, North used 'helping Rigby' as an excuse not to be alone with Denise. While I was happy to be a distraction, I was also anxious to bring up what exactly was going on between them. Clearly, there was some unfinished business and it felt like somehow the Parktown marching band was going to get caught up in the middle. As much as I wanted North to confront her, somewhere buried deep, I was worried they would get back together. So, I settled for attention from my crush, can you blame me?

Pushing the personal drama out of my head, I brought down my hands for the last run through of our rehearsal before we went to the review and felt pretty damn good. We weren't at the level of the best bands in the county, but I think we were definitely going to make some people take notice. The color guard had settled down to choreography that actually looked like normal and added to our show, and while we hadn't started adding things like horn flashes or fancy stepping, the core of each movement was solid. The playing and technique were there and the show was definitely at a respectable technical level.

While the band walked off the field to pack up their equipment, I twirled my whistle and realized perhaps my efforts of the past two weeks had been a little selfish. I hadn't added much to what had just taken place on the field. Realizing I had somewhat reverted to the leadership of last year by being more involved with myself and less with the band wasn't my proudest moment. Sure, I was still the first arrive and the last to leave, but my behavior struck me that maybe my crush was going a little bit obsessive and needed to be either called off or significantly reined in. In two weeks, my lack of responsibility hadn't yet had a direct negative impact, but I felt I was going to have to change something if we were going to be competitive later in the season. Walking to the pit, I grabbed a cymbal stand and walked towards the school with a lot on my mind.

It was the following day after school and we were already off to a difficult start. First, we'd had a rather disastrous inspection (it seemed the majority of the freshman class had forgotten to pack black socks). I was included in this debacle – shipping on the new drum major uniform Ms. Jenkins had ordered special for me had been delayed, leaving me in a lame mash up of concert dress. Although it was silly, I felt completely out of place and hated that I didn't match the rest of the band. Not to mention, I, among others, misplaced my gloves and we had to frantically search the school to come up with enough for everyone. Not to mention a few minor disasters with loading the equipment. For awhile, it had been touch and go about fitting the grand marimba in with everything else. We had finally loaded onto our three yellow school buses to head over to the review, and heads counts were being taken. I had walked in front of the bus looking for Manuel (a particularly precocious freshmen) when I heard North's raised voice. As I peeked around the bus, I saw North basically cornered by Denise. His body language made it abundantly clear he wanted to be anywhere else, enforced by the exclamation, "You have got to stop following me!"

"No! You haven't given me five minutes since I got here, and even that was band related. You're going to have to talk to me sooner or later."

"Denise, I thought I made it abundantly clear – I don't want you in my life anymore. I'm not sure why you thought following me here would do anything, but I wish you would just leave me alone!" North used a tone of voice I had never heard before.

Walking around the bus to end their conversation, I realized North and Denise's 'discussion' had been in plain view of the entire band waiting on the busses. Thus far, I was the only one who knew (well, Jude knew as well, but that's because I didn't keep anything from him) of the torrid back story between our two instructors. Unfortunately, this little scene was doing nothing to help the band, who was already on edge about the performance. Watching the instructors blow up at each other wouldn't help ease the frazzled nerves.

"It's time to go," I said.

"Fine!" North stormed past me towards his bus, while Denise turned towards hers.

I sighed and turned to walk to my own bus. As soon as I got on board my own bus, I was inundated with questions about what exactly had been going on outside. I pulled my headphones on quickly and listened to the show, trying to lose myself in it entirely, and ignore the sinking feeling I had in the bottom of my stomach.

Disaster.

That was the only word that could describe our performance. The show had been a perfect example of old school Parktown and I couldn't be more devastated. From the back of the field, Everett kept up solid and steady quarter notes to get everyone off the field as fast as possible, for which I was very grateful. Because we were the second band to perform, the crowd, not warmed up yet, clapped politely, obviously disinterested in our 'performance.' I could tell no one had been paying attention after the first major bout of phasing, nor the point where half the band had been off step, or the instance where a flag had nearly decapitated a saxophone. The show had been basically 'How Not to Perform' and I wondered if it was possible to die from embarrassment. My embarrassment was so bad, I contemplated if anyone would notice if I got off the podium during the show.

As I tried my best choke back the tears that were rapidly forming, it occurred to me the performance wasn't something that could be instantly forgotten and swept under the rug. Instead, not only would we have to watch the horrible event over and over, we would have to listen to the tapes the following day. It wasn't as if the performance had been a complete surprise. Ending with our blow up between the instructors, there were numerous reasons why the show had been as bad as it had. Although we all tried to ignore it, on top of everything, we had a truly terrible warm up in which no one seemed to want to get in tune. Adding to the trouble, North was busy running around trying to locate a spare bass drum head for our bottom bass. I was distracted, and, having never paid attention in the past, was totally unsure as to what I was supposed to do as drum major before a performance. Other than conduct our warm ups, I'm sure I looked lost and totally lacking in confidence – not exactly the best thing for the underclassmen to see.

Back at the truck, everyone was quiet as we packed up, and I debated whether or not we should ask Ms. Jenkins if we could just go ahead and leave the site altogether. Every other performance tonight would be a reminder in how we had utterly and totally failed. Furthermore, as transparent as my disappointed feelings were, I knew if I made some sort of speech my words would fall flat, so I did my best to individually talk to people about their performance – mainly, to listen. These small conversations kept me busy the rest of the night as I made my way through the sections. By listening to the Parktown band members, I started to feel better, because I wasn't alone – everyone felt the same way I did. Everyone felt deeply responsible for our failure. In that, I knew there was hope we would be able to come together and move past this performance. Although slightly petty, I also found solace in realizing our program wasn't the only one that could use work. While no one matched our total breakdown, there were a few that were close.

Contemplative on our ride home, it was easy to come to my next decision – no more North. It was as simple as that. I didn't have the time, effort, or energy to put into my crush that I didn't see going anywhere, especially when it was painfully obvious that my band needed me. The reality of my choice made me sad, but I knew it was necessary.

Back at Parktown, I carefully avoided both North and Denise and after an extended conversation with a still optimistic Ms. Jenkins, as usual, I was last to walk out to the parking lot. As I walked on complete autopilot to my usual parking space, I realized my car was missing.

"Jude..." I said aloud.

This instance wouldn't be the first time that my brother, the modern day Casanova, would take our car and forget to tell me. Sure enough, my cell phone beeped with an incoming text.

>> *Can you catch a ride home? I owe you...*

I laughed, because, what else was there to do? Somehow, my current situation seemed a perfect ending to my entirely crappy day. Stuck by myself in the empty parking lot, I started jamming Jude's speed dial into my phone to hopefully interrupt whatever romantic liaison he was in the middle of, when I noticed the parking lot wasn't completely empty. North's motorcycle was in its usual place.

"Rigby? Is that you?" North's voice sounded across the pavement.

Away from the bright lights of a football stadium, it was one of those totally dark nights where the moon had completely waned and the stars were covered by clouds. I hesitated a moment before putting my phone away and answering, "Umm, yeah?"

"What are you doing out here?"

"Waiting on my ride?" I answered unconvincingly.

"You drove here."

"Oh yeah."

I could hear his steps getting closer, and reminded myself he was no longer North – hottest instructor alive, but instead, Mr. Buchanan, helpful person affiliated with my marching band and of absolutely no interest to yours truly.

"Look, Rigby, this isn't exactly where I planned on having this conversation, but I've been trying to find you all night. I know you want to blame yourself—"

"Because it's all my fault!"

I heard North take a deep breath before he answered calmly, "How? How is it one person's fault if the entire band falls apart? Tell me."

My unshed tears from earlier in the evening swelled up again, and I was glad for the dark as I wiped them away, "It just is. You wouldn't understand."

"I wouldn't?" He paused a moment before continuing, "I saw you talking to the band tonight, and I'm sure at some point you realized it's not any one person's fault, yours included. Now, I've been down this road before and it's not going to help anyone if you try to take all the blame. A real leader moves on and learns from their mistakes. Lead by example, Rigby, show this band that yes, there is room for improvement, but true change has to come from the whole group. One person cannot transformation everything – no matter how much they want to."

He took a step closer and said, "Either way, I'm still proud of you. I saw you up there and you tried everything to hold it together."

"Thanks." Scuffing my Tom on the asphalt, I said, "On a scale of 1 to 10, how bad was it?"

My question sparked a smile, and I was glad North appreciated my reference to a joke we had started early on. After a given run through of the show, practice or otherwise, he would give me an arbitrary number on a point system that seemed to make no sense.

Cocking his head to the side, he appeared to think very seriously about his answer and then said, "2.5."

We had not yet broken 5.0. I wondered what a 10 performance would sound like.

North continued, "Now, as much as I want to believe you, I don't think anyone is coming to pick you up. Can I give you a ride home?"

North was right next to me, but I could only see the outline of his face. There was no way to determine what his expression was. Was he asking me to be polite? Was he asking me because he felt sorry for me? Why was he asking?

"I..."

I was only human.

"I..."

I would probably never get this chance again.

"I..."

I didn't see Denise anywhere.

"...thanks. That would be great."

"Come on then, hop on."

Chapter 10: Shut Up and Drive

If I knew how much getting on the back of North's motorcycle would alter the rest of my year, I don't know if I would've hopped on behind him.   Although I had imagined it a million times, up until this moment, I didn't think I would ever actually get the chance to be so physically close to North.   While this situation was hypothetically crossing an invisible line I think we both knew was present, I guess it could still be argued he was simply giving me a ride home.   Quite honestly, while I desperately wanted the gesture to be more, I didn't want to come off as an immature high school student, so I forced myself not to over think things.

We walked over to his bike silently and I was glad I decided to leave most of my marching related stuff inside Ms. Jenkins's office.   Also, as we neared where the old Honda was parked, it occurred to me I had no idea how to even get on a motorcycle, let alone be a passenger.   I started to doubt my decision.

"Just give me a chance to crank it.   Sorry I don't have helmets, I kind of left in a hurry today.   I promise you'll be safe."

With an easy and effortless motion, North kicked back the stand, then slid onboard and started up his bike.

This was it. I could still back out. I could still call my parents to come and get me. I could still...always wonder what would've happened. With the engine revving, North offered his hand and said, "Come on."

With a lot less grace, I found myself on the back of the bike. Thoughts of the performance vanished from my head and the frustration from the evening quickly melted away — all I knew was the incredible feeling and rush of being close to North. In that instant, I could completely understand why Denise wasn't going to give him up with a fight. Being with Everett had rarely made me feel this good. In fact, there were very few things I could come up with at this moment that had ever made me feel this way.

Bringing him even closer into my personal space, North half turned around and questioned, "So, first time on a bike?"

I nodded, unable to concentrate on much more than his face was mere inches from mine.

He continued, "Given we don't have protection for our heads, I'm not going to go that fast, but basically, just lean when I lean, and hold on. I've been driving this thing for a long time, so I'm not some sort of rookie."

His instructions didn't sound that difficult, and I especially liked the part where I was literally told to make physical contact with him.

"Got it," I answered.

"Where do you live?"

Knowing he was new to town, I asked, "Do you know where Birch Tree Park is?"

"Yes."

"The neighborhood right after it — by the pond."

"Alright — mind if we take the long way?"

My parents knew I was at the band thing tonight, and for maybe the first time ever, I was going to take advantage of their trust and, as North so eloquently put it, 'take the long way.'

"Not at all."

He moved to go forward, then looked over his shoulder at me and said, "This is the part where you hang on."

So, that's what I did. I put my arms around his waist and held tight. As the vast majority of my male interaction primarily involved Everett (which I had promptly forgotten in the months since our break up), being so near a male – especially North – was almost my undoing. Not helping any was the fact there was definitely some ab definition under my hands. Although my mind had other ideas, I had to physically restrain myself from not completely pressing up against North's broad back. I forced a small space between us...or, at least, I tried to. I couldn't be certain, but it seemed North had other ideas, or maybe I was just reading into things, but I could swear he sped up, taking turns fluidly and forcing me to hold on tighter. Not that I minded in the least.

Under the moonless sky – we were off across town. Given it was September, the weather pattern was still warm, but as we increased in speed, I was glad for North's radiating body heat. I thought a lot as we sped along through the night. I thought about how different this felt from being with Everett. I had always found my ex-boyfriend attractive, but not in the all encompassing way I was feeling now. Everett was comfortable, but North seemed to spark a side of me I didn't even know existed.

We didn't talk. We couldn't have anyway with the wind rushing past, but I hoped the connection I was feeling wasn't all in my head. If it was, and all I was going to get was this one ride, well, I was going to make tonight count. The sites of Parktown flew past me and I almost laughed at how surreal the whole scene seemed.

This couldn't be my life, could it?

Finally, far too soon, we reached my house. Pulling into the driveway, I noticed Jude had already parked the car. Funny to think how just a half hour ago, his taking our ride had totally frustrated me – now I couldn't be happier for the inconvenience. North quickly cut the engine and I hoped my parents weren't awake or listening to know I had been dropped off in a motorcycle. Using North's shoulders to steady myself, I swung my leg over the seat and got off the bike. And there it was – the tension wasn't my imagination!

"So…" I stepped back and stuck my hands in my pockets "Thanks."

"Don't mention it. You were a good passenger."

This was supposed to be the part where I walked inside and ignored the spark between us, but I found my feet were literally glued to the spot. I didn't want this time to end. Here we were, just a guy and girl, not an instructor and a student, or years apart, or any of that.

"I—"

"So—"

"You go first," said North, ever the gentleman.

I didn't want to. I didn't want to open my mouth and pour out my feelings and risk being stepped all over and turned down. As much as I was going to regret not saying anything, I was able to convince myself it wasn't like I was walking away empty handed from the evening. The ride to my house was something I could always remember. Completely losing my confidence, I finally answered, "Oh, um, I just wanted to say thanks for all your help with the band. Contrary to tonight's performance, you are making a big difference."

"Oh…"

Was it my overactive imagination, or did he sound disappointed?

"Well, guess I'll see you tomorrow," I said and began walking to the garage door.

In my delusional state, I hesitated, waiting for some sweeping romantic gesture, but North wasn't getting off of his bike, so I very slowly shuffled towards the house – just in case he changed his mind. I was about half way when I heard him say, "Rigby, wait—"

I instantly turned around, but whatever North was going to say or do, he was cut off as Jude opened the side door and walked over to our car. North and I locked eyes and both recognized the moment was over.

"Hey Rig, do you know where, oh…"

My brother was instantly aware of his faux pas, but there was no way of undoing what he had done.

"I should be going," he said and all but ran back inside.

I wanted to simultaneously maim my brother and plead for North to stay, but I didn't get a chance to do either. North quickly started up the bike and sped away, while Jude looked at me and started laughing hysterically.

"What's so funny?" I growled.

"I never expected to cock block my own sister."

"Yeah, well, you did."

"Was that the instructor?"

"What are you, the valedictorian or something?" I answered sarcastically.

Jude paused a moment, before he responded, "Sis, look, I really am sorry, y'know taking the car and well, interrupting your little after hours 'practice session' or whatever…"

Ignoring his dig, I said lightly, "I should probably be thanking you, without your taking the car, I never would've been on that bike in the first place."

Jude wrapped a friendly arm around me as we walked into the house, "You're probably right."

Whether my brother was correct or not, and whether or not it was healthy to drop a crush like North overnight, I forced myself to stick to my new plan the next day. I spent the afternoon struggling not to think about my instructor and what almost happened with him. Instead, I went over the tapes, generating a large, long list of improvements for the band, with goals for myself and my direction as well. The thing was – as I watched the band over and over and over again – I noticed the show was salvageable. Underneath everything that had gone wrong, I heard clear notes and witnessed some good marching technique. There was hope, and that's all I needed.

After school on Thursday, I asked North and Ms. Jenkins if I could personally address the band after we watched and listened to the tapes as a group. They agreed. North looked like he had something more to discuss with me, but declined to say anything further. I was glad. As far as I was concerned, Tuesday night was some sort of fluke and mostly in my imagination. I didn't need to talk to North to hear his version of letting me down gently.

"Rigby?" Ms. Jenkins asked as we watched North leave the room.

"Yes?" I answered, inwardly panicking, thinking she had somehow found out of North driving me home.

"I have a surprise for you."

My band director's voice was neutral, such that I couldn't tell if what she was about to tell me was good or bad.

"Yes?" I asked timidly.

"You're uniform finally arrived!" Ms. Jenkins clapped her hands together and I breathed a sigh of relief. Gesturing to a uniform bag and shoe box, she said, "It's right here."

With my heart rate only just slowing down, I managed to reply, "I'll get them after practice. Are we ready to watch the show?"

"I've got them all cued up."

After the tapes were viewed and listened to in complete silence, I stepped up to the director's podium, took a deep breath and announced, "There's no point in watching that tape ever again, because we are never going to let that happen again. Now, I talked to a number of you and I think what happened on the field comes down to two things: lack of confidence and lack of experience. I'm not sure why we weren't confident – we have an awesome show – the best show I've ever marched. We also have, for the first time ever, two instructors to make us better. So, there, if you don't believe it, then trust me, because I can see the whole field at once and what we're capable of – this is a great marching program. This brings me to lack of experience. Sure, most of the bands we saw on Tuesday have been competitive for years, and maybe, they have more people that have marched an actual show in front of others before, but, and freshmen, I'm talking to you – this is your chance to show people they are wrong about your class. Furthermore, it's not like you are without any experience – you've been marching all summer."

I paused for just a moment to let my words sink in, before I concluded, "So, our first competition is in a little less than a month. In that time, I think we can get some things done...both on the field and off, starting with the game on Friday. We're playing Harrison-Benavidez, and you know they have one of the best marching programs in the region. I want you to pay careful attention to how they do everything. I will be doing the same. Look at the group when they are at attention and when they are not. Watch their marching style. What do they do that puts them ahead? How can we incorporate what they do? At the same time, don't be too intimidated by them. At one point, they were where we are now."

I started passing out a photocopied list of my list of improvements around the band.

"So, guys, this is a comprehensive checklist of everything from that video. It's a place to start and I'm sure each of you can think of one thing that you can do better next time. Let's get out and get busy. Sectionals first, then full practice in an hour. Remember, we can do this!"

My excited band members hurried out of the room. I wasn't far behind them, mostly because I was still trying to avoid any solitary conversation or time with North. I saw him try to catch my attention, but ignored him and headed to my poor neglected woodwinds – the top section on my list. Lieutenant Emma brightened when she saw me, and the rest of the flutes, piccolos, clarinets and saxophones she was with snapped to attention.

"No pressure, I just wanted to see what you were practicing."

Emma's usually happy face turned dark and stormy, and she said, "Well, we call it Unlucky Charms."

I knew immediately what she was talking about, most especially because I had been hearing about this part personally from the members of the section, and also from the judges on the tape. For some reason, Ms. Jenkins had selected an incredibly difficult piece for our third song, and the hardest part fell on the high woodwinds. They not only had to simultaneously play all these difficult runs, but they had to do so very loudly, and complete a crazy drill move. They hadn't perfected the notes yet, but I wasn't blaming them.

"So, let's break it down together."

And that's what we did. We started in eight count sets at very slow tempos and gradually got faster. By the time our hour had passed, we were closing in on the actual tempo, and I think everyone felt much better about the situation. The great thing about working with underclassmen was the instant and total respect they gave me. Even though I couldn't play their instruments and no idea what it was like to cut off the tips of my gloves, there was a great level of discipline that I appreciated.

After ignoring North's further attempts to make conversation, I scooted home and relaxed by trying on my drum major uniform. Ms. Jenkins, for whatever reason, had let me pick what I wanted to wear from the Band Shoppe catalogue over the summer. Instead of inheriting Marti's old uniform, which probably wouldn't have fit me anyway, I appreciated the choice. There were an infinite number of options, and I knew when I found the style, that it was truly 'me.' Still in its plastic, I unzipped the coat cover and looked fondly at the uniform that would carry me through my final season. Being the first to wear it, I honestly believed there was no previous luck (bad or good) associated with the garment. I was the one who would be putting my mark on it and right now I was convinced it was going to be a good one.

Holding up the polyester in the mirror against myself, I was pleased with the reflection. I had gone for an old school majorette look, and after checking out the other drum majors at the review, knew no one had anything like I'd be wearing. Our school colors weren't the easiest to combine, but I loved how the deep purple and silver worked together. The violet skirt was full and ended just below my knees, and the jacket had a formal military feel – overall, it was an awesome combination of pretty and powerful. Paired with a pair of stacked white boots and a black Aussie with a flamboyant purple plume, I felt the part when the entire ensemble was put together. Even with everything that had happened in the past week, I still felt optimistic. I was ready to face Harrison-Benavidez and whatever else the season wanted to throw at me. For the first time since seeing my name on the list in the band room, I truly felt I had earned the mantle of Parktown drum major.

Chapter 11: Atonal

There was a good energy as I entered the band room on Friday afternoon. For once, I wasn't the first person there, but that was mostly because I had forced myself to leave later so I would avoid North. I know, not my proudest moment. However, I swear my heart actually yearned when I saw his motorcycle in the parking lot. Of course, my yearning quickly turned to something a lot less healthy as I looked and saw Denise's perfect little coupe parked next to it.

Shaking my rather immature yearning aside, and threw myself into greeting the Parktown band members, trying to get them pumped for our performance in a few hours. In my past seasons, I usually just hung out with the rest of the drumline in the percussion room and pretty much ignored everyone else. Now, I was like a member of student government or something, getting out and greeting my constituents. There were nerves, for sure, and I would be lying if I didn't group myself in the anxious and edgy category, but overall, I think my worries were outweighed by anticipation. Cautiously optimistic, everyone was eager to see if we could bounce back from Tuesday's terrible performance. After checking in with as many people as I could, I brought my band leadership together for a short pre-trip meeting in Ms. Jenkins' office.

"Okay, I hope you've all been helping with uniform inspection and instrument checks. We don't want to get to HB and be missing a sousaphone or something."

The group nodded, so I continued, "So guys, I think the usual thing is during the third quarter we go over and make nice with the kids from the other band. Isn't that how it goes?"

I got a lot of blank looks, mostly because, well, none of us knew what we were doing. We were all brand new to our positions, and previously, our behavior wouldn't have mattered. We probably would've just headed straight for the concession stand and not thought anything more about it. Tonight, I was determined the change I wanted would start at the games. I wanted the rest of the band to see we were taking things seriously, and if this was what winning and successful band members did, then gosh darn it, we were going to do the same.

I closed my comments by saying, "Anyway, let's be respectful and polite and see what they have to say. Maybe they'll have some good advice for our band!"

Too bad I had no idea these would be my famous last words.

What happened during the third quarter was nothing short of total and utter embarrassment.

Everything had been going well. We performed excellently. The crowd had been totally involved in our show, and from that, the band members responded until we finished to a loud round of applause. Now, for our little group, I was proud of where we had come from and what we had done. We marched off onto the track, so we could see the home band's performance. For the first time since Tuesday, I found myself actively seeking North.

His was the opinion I needed to hear, because I knew he wouldn't lie to me. While I felt good about things, he would tell me if I had just imagined our great show.

While the Harrison-Benavidez high school marching Marauders, all two hundred of them got set, I asked, "How was it?"

"Rigby, we need to talk—"

"We can talk about that later," I interrupted and continued, "What I need to know is was the show as good as I thought it was?"

Even though I was standing next to him, I risked a look to meet his face, and saw his insanely blue eyes twinkling back at me, "Yes, Rigby, it was good. You weren't imagining things. But—"

"Thank you."

That was all I needed to hear. Now, I could go with my head held high to our third quarter conversation. I wanted to move away from North, but it was like I had been snared in his devastating good looks tractor beam and found myself unable to walk away. Together, we watched Harrison-Benavidez perform in companionable silence. I was grateful North seemed to understand this was the wrong place to discuss what may or may not have happened the other night. His comfortable presence was the kind of closeness that once upon a time I had felt with Everett. I wondered if North felt the connection too. Abruptly, I brought my deceitful thoughts back around and concentrated on the marching band in front of us. Interestingly, I saw a band that was definitely good, but not unbeatable. In fact, while I noticed the band, the thing that struck me were the drum majors.

They weren't exactly...together. Well, two of them were in (mostly) perfect sync, and one of them appeared to be a beat or two behind. The miscommunication wasn't completely obvious, but to me, the discordance stuck out. The side of the band she was helping with was also a bit behind, which convinced me I was hearing what

I was seeing. While I didn't want to sit and judge, somehow this little moment made me feel better. It made me realize everyone can have an off day. I wanted to ask North if he saw the mistake too, but Denise had already leeched herself onto his other side, and I didn't want to get involved in a conversation with them.

As their show, a tribute to Queen, came to a triumphant end, I quickly gathered up Emma, Adelaide, Everett, and Todd, and together we walked over to the home side of the field. Stepping into enemy territory, my Spidey senses started to tingle, and for some reason, at that exact moment, I realized how fiercely protective and proud of my band I was.

It wasn't difficult to find the Harrison-Benavidez band members – the large mass of maroon and white polyester easily stuck out among the crowd. I had noted what the drum majors were wearing during their performance, and made my way through the group to where I thought I glimpsed their leadership.

As we walked, I could tell most of their band members were totally judgmental against out little party, which, after the week I had, I really did not need. Especially given the fact I knew we had performed a good show. Sure, our previous reputation and terrible performance at the review weren't helping our image, but whatever happened to band geek solidarity? Weren't we all on the same team? Why weren't people coming up and saying 'good job' or 'way to improve'? Was that so hard to do?

When we finally got through to the band leaders, I managed to make eye contact with one of the drum majors – the snarky auburn haired one – and then she did the unthinkable – she looked the other way. Like, pretended I wasn't even there. The slight was so quick, I don't think anyone noticed. If I had been a cartoon character, this would've been the point where steam would've been coming out of my ears. I was usually easy going, but as defensive as I was about my group, my hands clenched. As they closed the circle and turned their backs on us, my little group, outcasts in a sea of maroon were left just standing there. Then Everett put a hand on my shoulder, and shook his head slightly. I shook my head back at him. No one was going to treat me and my band that way. No one. I don't care how many trophies they had. I marched up and tapped one of the drum majors on the shoulder, "Excuse me?"

She turned around, saw who I was, and asked in an annoyed tone, "Yes? Can I help you with something? Are you lost?"

Shocked at her rudeness, I was unable to speak.

"Nice hat, by the way," one of the co-drum majors said with a smirk.

Even if my Aussie was a bit over the top, I completely loved it. Furthermore, you insult my hat, you insult me. I cleared my throat and then announced loudly, "If you can't get your little wonder trio together, how do you expect to get your band together?"

My voice was raised. I didn't care. She, of the auburn hair, looked shocked, which, to be sure, the rest of my little group did as well. I was even a bit unsure of where my rage had come from. When no one said anything, I continued, "We may not be as loud as you, or as big as you, but guess what we do have? Manners," I stumbled over my words, "...and heart. So, you can take your crap conducting, formulaic show and we'll see you on the field in a few weeks!"

When my Parktown friends failed to do anything, I snapped my fingers ala Ferris Bueller and got the hell out of there. As we all but pushed our way out of the section, I already heard the whispers ripple through their band, 'Did she just say what I think she said?' 'Who was that girl?' 'Is she from Parktown?'

Just fabulous, this wonderful moment of unprovoked antagonism was to be my legacy – not of bringing back

Parktown from the depths of the judges low scores, but instead, for being a genuine (and probably uncalled for) bully.

We returned in silence. Whether or now my section leaders were afraid of me or not, I didn't want to dwell on what had just happened. Back on our side of the field I waited for the inevitable shame-fest I thought was coming, and when it didn't, I was surprised. Maybe my little group was scared of me – not that I could blame them, I think maybe I was just a little bit scared of myself at the moment. More than anything, I wanted to march straight back to the buses and start working on a Universal Remote so I could start the week over again (and maybe just stay paused on Tuesday night forever), but I didn't get that far. Instead, what happened was Everett marched me right over to the drumline and proceeded to brag to them what had I done. As he completely embellished the events of what had occurred, I realized, if yelling at a complete stranger was all it took to get him to talk to me again, I would've done this a long time ago! Out of nowhere, a big weight lifted from my shoulders and I easily interacted with my old section. I guess I had completely underrated normalcy. Settling in to relive Everett's interpretation of my rage, I felt that this was how my senior year was supposed to be.

When the referee's whistle blew to mark the end of the fourth quarter, I heard some outrageous rumors circulating through the Parktown band. They ranged from I had used my Aussie in a very unladylike manner upon one of the HB drum majors, to other possibilities of me and the section leaders being involved in some sort of Sharks vs. the Jets ala West Side Story. The true story was I had gone way outta line and there was no way to undo what I had so foolishly done. I could only hope Ms. Jenkins didn't get wind of my behavior and ban me from future games. I wasn't exactly putting forth a positive image for the Parktown marching program. Furthermore, without a co-drum major, there wasn't anyone I could hide behind. Everett's acceptance of me notwithstanding, there was definitely more intelligent courses of action I could've chosen to do.

I kept outside the buses long enough to see everyone safely loaded and got on at the last minute taking a front seat, where I hoped I could ignore further comments and questions.

It turned out I was not to be so lucky.

"So, anything you want to talk about?" A cocky grinned North asked me, sliding in next to me and trapping me in the seat with him.

Maybe he hadn't heard what I had done.

"Not particularly," I answered breezily.

"Nothing at all?"

The bus sputtered and pulled away from Harrison-Benavidez high school. I was glad I was never going to see the place again. I finally answered, "I take it you heard about my 'comments.'"

"Well, yes, but that's not what I was talking about."

"Oh."

He looked around, but there was no one paying attention to us. As with most dark and long rides across the district, my classmates seemed to content to indulge in quieter conversations. With our energy well spent from the long week, there were no sing-alongs or shouting the show (or previous shows) at the top of our lungs.

In a quiet tone, North said, "About the other night. I think there are a few things you should know about."

I was immediately torn. I desperately wanted North to open up to me and to learn all about what the heck Denise had been talking about, but I knew once I invited him in on that level, then there wasn't going to be any room left for the band.

I held up my hand to interrupt him and said, "Look, North, I think we should just leave things at that one night, and our relationship as it is — you're the band's instructor, and I'm their drum major. We're not friends, or anything more."

North was caught off guard.

"Is that how you really feel?"

I looked away, unable to meet his stare and said, "It is."

"Okay, Rigby. If that's how you want it."

I wasn't surprised when he got up to leave the seat.

I sighed and slumped down. I had just blown my one and only chance to start anything with North. What I had said was in direct conflict with how I felt. I wanted to tell him riding on the back of the bike was one of the coolest things I had ever done in my eighteen years. I wanted to tell him I had total respect for him for staying out of Denise's clutches. I wanted to tell him he was quite possibly one of the greatest people I had ever met — that he was nice, genuine, and loyal — everything I found attractive in a person. I wanted to tell him that wasn't how I felt at all...but remained silent.

Chapter 12: Just So We're Clear

"And that was how I made a fine mess of things."

"Seriously, sis, but has anyone ever told you that you take things way too seriously."

"Seriously?" I asked, smiling at Jude.

He didn't return the smile, but said, "Because, in case you missed it, you just missed your big moment. You totally shut him down."

"I guess that's a new habit of mine," I responded, thinking of Everett and my horrible treatment of him earlier in the year.

"Is that what you meant to do?"

"'Is that what you meant to do?'" I mocked back at him, and continued in what I hoped was a convincing tone, "Of course it was."

"Ten bucks says you are dating this North dude by the end of the season."

I literally laughed in my brother's face. Nothing sounded more ridiculous to me. I asked, "Didn't you just tell me I shut him down?"

"Yup."

"And why do girls at our school find you attractive?"

"That is entirely too complicated a concept for you to understand, sister dear. Anyway, we were talking about you. Now, since you're going to end up with North, care to enlighten me as to how you're going to get around the, ahem, illegal aspects of your being together?"

"What do you mean?"

"He is your teacher, is he not?"

"Sort of." Even in my daydreams, actually dating North was always tinged by the cloud of how much trouble we could both get in.

"I'm not sure the county would see if that way."

"What would you do?"

"I thought things weren't going to happen between the two of you?"

"But if they did…"

"I think you need to be smart."

"How?"

"Stay off the grid. Keep all communication between you two in person. If you have some giant texting session or an e-mail trail, well…it could end up bad for both of you."

"Yeah, that makes sense."

"But you weren't going to do that, were you?"

I would not tell Jude of the very few texts I had from North on my phone. Sure – they were all related to practice or marching or links about band, but I had read and re-read them, searching for any additional message he might be trying to send. I would also not inform my brother how I agonized over my responses. I responded casually, "No."

"Good. Now, I know you're a big girl and all that – but I have to ask, he's not taking advantage of you or anything, is he?"

"Jude!"

"Rigby!" He said in the same high pitched tone I had used, then lowered his voice and continued, "I'm your brother, I have to ask these things."

"Younger brother."

"By five minutes."

I looked into my brother's face, a similar more masculine version of my own, and said, "I promise – nothing, untoward is going on."

"You'll let me know if it does?"

"Ew, but yes." Although we had a good relationship, and I was grateful for Jude in my life, I probably didn't tell him enough. Even though it was tough for me to say, I murmured, "Thanks."

"Anytime."

We spent the first half hour watching the tape from Friday night at practice on Tuesday. I actually got chills during the ballad. The band was so proud of themselves that they were cheering along with the audience at the end. This response was perhaps the first time something even remotely similar had occurred in the Parktown band room. If this was last season, everyone would be showing up to practice late and we sure as heck wouldn't be watching our performance, much less cheering for our efforts.

Instead, everyone had been promptly waiting to the tape to begin, and I overheard active discussions between members about what they could personally do to make their show better. Of course, I also heard a few comments about my interaction with the drum majors of HB, but I chose to flat out ignore them and continue with my business. And speaking of business, that's all I was getting from North. From the time he exited the bus on Friday night, to my current interaction with him, his attitude was all very official. There were no more smiles or inside jokes, and I found myself missing them. Had I done the wrong thing? Was there room in my life for both something with North and being Parktown's drum major? Could I have phrased things differently? What did I know about relationships anyway? I'd had approximately one serious one in my entire life. Furthermore, what could come of me dating North anyway? Scanning the band room and feeling the collective energy that was going through it, I told myself it was okay I had chosen my band, and had to believe my options were a one or the other kind of decision.

Ms. Jenkins made some encouraging remarks, and then the band broke for short sectionals. This time would give the section leaders some space to address those things that pertained to their instrumentalists or performers specifically, before we all gathered together to start running through the show.

My first stop was to the color guard – a group I had definitely been neglecting. After watching the tape, they were top of my list. Actually, I knew I was overdue in spending time with Adelaide and her girls. Although Denise had made progress with the most eclectic group in the band, the routine for the closer was not that great. In my mind, the flags should be an interpretation of the notes and rhythms we were playing, and thus far, the two did not match up. The current choreography seemed more distracting than anything else. It was a delicate situation, and one I wanted to handle on my own. I didn't want to involve North, because, quite honestly, I didn't want him to spend any additional time with Denise, which was pretty selfish considering I had purposely distanced myself from him.

Walking through the hallways of the school, I wondered, at this point, what was stopping me know from fully supporting these two getting back together? Hadn't Denise sacrificed a lot to be with North? Didn't she deserve a second chance? But there was still something that wouldn't let me agree with the pair. She was wrong for him, and not just because she had cheated on him. It was more than that. He needed someone different...

...someone like me.

I stopped walking. Drastically changing my mind and its traitorous thoughts, I decided to clear my head by walking and conducting the show. Sure, I looked weird, but it was hard to think of anything else with the movements running through my head. Feeling better, I gathered my courage and walked over to make nice with the color guard instructor. Although we had never explicitly talked about it, I knew she knew that I liked North and so far in the season it had all kinds of awkward between us. The only reason I was actively approaching her was because it was for the overall good of my band. However, before I could open my mouth to speak, Denise folded one arm across her chest and began inspecting her manicure.

"So, North told me all about your little 'ride' last week." Her tone insinuated how unimpressed she was. Before I even had a chance to form a response, she continued, "Did you honestly think that meant something?"

Even if I did think it had meant something (which deep down I thought it had), all was negated by the fact he had told his ex-girlfriend about what I thought had been a private moment. If the ride had been really special, he wouldn't have shared it with anyone...well, maybe if he had a twin brother or something...but definitely not his ex-girlfriend.

Crossing my arms across my chest, I answered, "No, it was just a friendly ride home, why would it mean anything?"

I hoped my voice was convincing, but I didn't think I was fooling either of us.

"Good, I just wanted to make sure we were on the same page."

Was this a challenge? The same thing that wouldn't let me go on Friday night came back again and I asked, "What page is that?"

I was hoping I had called her bluff. I wanted to see if she would openly admit her feelings for North to me again.

"Listen, little miss drum major, what North and I had going on came along while you were still a miserable underclassmen, you wouldn't understand."

I contemplated my answer for a moment before I said, "I'll tell you what I do understand. I understand he hasn't looked at you since you got here, and he didn't mention you once before you got here. I understand you cheated on quite possibly the greatest guy in the world, and I understand you're doing a mediocre job with the color guard. I may only be in high school but I understand that much."

While maybe I momentarily took her by surprise, she spat back, "You don't know what you're talking about."

I shrugged my shoulders and walked away slowly, "You're probably right."

I stomped over to the band equally mad at myself for not sticking around to talk to the color guard about how we could improve their performance and for letting Denise get to me. Why did I even acknowledge her? Or show North's ex-girlfriend her words so obviously got to me? She obviously was trying to get to me with her snarky comments. Still, annoyed as I was, part of me was devastated – why had North told her about our ride?

I probably don't have to tell you that open animosity is not the most conducive environment to bringing a mediocre band to greatness. While I think Denise and I more or less tolerated each other before, I felt like now the battle was on in earnest. Ironically, the facts were: I didn't want to be with North (at the very least, I didn't want him to get back together with his former girlfriend) and Denise obviously did want him back. Neither of us knew what North wanted.

I moped around during sectionals and didn't feel at all like going through the show. Trying to convince myself

I would feel better after practice, I climbed the podium. As I brought my hands up to start the opener, I glanced behind me on the hill overlooking the practice field, noting instantly the color guard instructor pretty much could not stand any closer to North unless she took of residency in his lap. I gritted my teeth and began conducting the show.

I shouldn't have been surprised when North approached me after practice, "Rigby?"

I could tell from his tone of voice he was not in the mood for humor, and wasn't about to continue our long running joke of privately making fun of the trombones fashion sense.

"Yes?" I replied with an equally professional voice.

"Denise seems to think the reason the guard isn't together in the closer is because you're not conducting clearly."

With the exception of Tommy, who was a clarinet player during the concert season, most of the color guard weren't musicians and from what I could gather barely understood what my clearly defined downbeats looked like. I shot North a skeptical look and responded, "Really, she thinks that?"

From his barely contained eye roll, I sensed North was even less interested being caught in the middle of us than I did 'competing' with Denise in the first place.

"Apparently."

I literally had to bite my tongue to ask why she wasn't with us telling me her 'observation' to my face, but instead asked, "What do you think?"

"Is this about Friday night, because if it is—"

"Rigby?"

Saved by Everett. I don't think I had ever been happier to see someone than at that exact moment. I would've even taken Eleanor, the strangely always optimistic freshman.

"Yes?"

"Umm…"

Everett was smart enough to know he had run into the middle of something, and started backing away slowly. Seizing the opportunity, I latched onto Everett's arm, and followed him away from North.

"So, you wanted to talk to me about something?"

Everett gave me a weird look, but continued to walk with me. Once we were far enough away from North, he asked, "What's up with you two anyway?"

Unsure how much Everett had picked up on so far I decided it was probably best to feign complete ignorance and replied, "What are you talking about?"

"That was weird back there."

"What do you mean?"

"I thought you and North got along okay."

"Oh well, we do."

Everett didn't seem to believe me, and I could understand why. I wasn't really selling it.

"What did he mean about Friday night? Was he mad about the things you said to the Harrison-Benavidez drum majors? Because I can totally back you up on that."

"No," I said, trying desperately to come up with any topic North and I could've been discussing.

"Then what is it?"

The whole situation with North was not something I had shared with anyone besides Jude. I mean, why would I? A) Our relationship was not going anywhere and b) even if it could, there's still the whole fact North is our instructor. Still, with my ex-boyfriend in front of me, I had forgotten just how easy it was to talk to Everett. No matter our past, he knew me. You can't date someone for three years and not be intimately acquainted with their personality. With him, I didn't feel nervous, I felt relaxed and ever since North's introduction to my life, I hadn't felt that way.

"Umm…"

"Come on, Rig, you can tell me."

I paused for a moment before realizing, "I can, can't I? I mean, we are friends after all."

"Uhh, yeah."

"And friends tell each other things, right?"

"Sure."

I opened my mouth to speak, but actually forming the words was more difficult than I imagined. Finally, I put together the blindingly clear sentence, "Well, there was like almost a thing with um, North."

"What do you mean, 'a thing'?" Everett began tapping his foot, which I knew was his classic sign of annoyance.

"Er..."

"A 'thing' like we were a 'thing'?" His voice was strained.

Had I pushed things too far by telling Everett? A flash of Denise's smug face popped into my head and I decided, no, I hadn't. If North was sharing details about us, so could I. However, as my ex-boyfriend continued to look at me, I realized things were not going as I anticipated them. I thought Everett would be more of a friend, and maybe give me some much needed advice.

"No, maybe...I don't know."

"No offense, Rigby, but I think that's one of the things you either know of you don't."

"Actually I don't. Anyways, so what if it was?" I challenged.

"What would you see in him anyway?"

"Never mind, forget I said anything."

"Fine, I will."

And with that, Everett abruptly walked away.

"Just so we're clear, by choosing to fully support the band and hold back my interest in North, I have managed to alienate both the color guard instructor, and apparently the drumline section leader. Not to mention the fact North is apparently some kind of guy who likes to gossip with his ex-girlfriend."

"This is why I never joined band," Jude replied as he took a big drink of Gatorade, then continued, "Everything is entirely too complicated in your world. For me, it's easy, you run, and if you have the fastest time, then you win. You don't rely on anyone else – just yourself. Nothing else enters into the equation."

"What would you do if you were me?"

"What can you do?"

"I was thinking of not doing anything."

"Correct me if I'm wrong, sis, but I think this situation is going to require a little bit of proactivity on your part."

"That's just what I was afraid of."

"First of all, I have to question the intelligence of your telling Everett about North."

"Please don't remind me." On my way home from practice, it occurred to me that Everett knowing of my interest in North couldn't lead to anything good.

"Other than the fact, that, yes, you sort of got the last word about you two ever getting back together, why did you tell him?"

"I guess... Denise got to me more than I thought she did."

"Why?"

"You'll think I'm an idiot."

"Try me."

I hesitated, but decided to tell Jude. Somewhere between all his hook ups, I believed he was searching for the same spark I was – that romance wasn't dead.

"Fine – what you walked out on the other day in our driveway, I thought that meant something. Something he wouldn't talk to her about."

"How do you know he did?"

"She mentioned it."

"But in what context?"

"What are you trying to say, Jude?"

"Maybe you should talk to North and let him tell you exactly what he said. Could be you're jumping to conclusions."

"Could be. In the meantime, should I call Everett and ask him to forget what I told him this afternoon?"

"No. No, no, no, no, no."

"And why not?"

"You've already made a mistake, Rig, you don't need to draw extra attention to it. As illegal as you're interest in North may be, at this point nothing has happened. Keep it that way. Also, when it comes down to it, Everett is a good guy – he's not going to rat you out to your band director."

"True. I just hope he doesn't do anything else."

Chapter 13: Talk it Out

A strange weather front came through practically overnight and our Thursday practice was freakishly cold. It seemed fall arrived in a hurry and summer was well on its way out – nothing but a memory. Funny, how accurate the weather can be. I zipped my hoodie up and thought about texting Jude to bring me my scarf.

As I stretched out and observed the band, it didn't take book smarts like my brother's to know the bad feelings from both Denise and Everett had quickly translated into their sections. For all that my shouting at Harrison-Benavidez had brought us together; it seemed in the past two days we had regressed significantly. There wasn't an out and out revolution, per se, but there was animosity that hadn't been present previously. The passion which had been driving the band had inexplicably evaporated and was replaced by technically accurate notes, but a complete lack of enthusiasm. Temps dragged, drill was no longer precise and with the first competition rapidly approaching, I was stressed, and unsure of how to clear up the mess I hadn't realized I would make. Funny me, how I thought by taking a step back with North, a step forward in my friendship with Ev, and a step towards a better band with Denise my dream of a competitive band would all come together. Jude had encouraged me to confront all parties, but when I asked (begged) him to do it for me, he only smiled and shook his head.

I hated when he was right.

Little Emma, my dependable woodwind Lieutenant found me during one of the water breaks, a tradition we had started at the beginning of the school year. We rubbed our hands together for warmth and she asked, "So, what's up?"

I could tell she was trying to be casual, but at the same time it was obvious she wanted to tell me something. I said, "What do you mean?"

Refusing to make eye contact, she answered, "I've heard a few things."

"Like what?"

"Specifically?"

"Well, first there's Everett..." she said, finally looking at me.

"First? What do you mean by 'first?'"

"Umm..." The poor girl looked supremely uncomfortable, and I had to remind myself I was basically yelling at a sophomore who seemed to always be on my side. It had probably taken most of her courage to come up and deliver whatever bad news she had.

"I'm sorry," I replied, controlled my breathing and continued, "Rough week. What did Everett say?"

"Youtriedtogetbacktogetherwithhim."

"Slower, please, it sounded like you said that I..."

"—tried to get back together with him."

"I did?!" I forced my voice lower and said, "When did this happen exactly?"

"You mean, you didn't?"

"No, definitely not..." In that moment I understood what my crafty ex-boyfriend was attempting. He was trying to force my hand to make me admit there was no way I was trying to get back together with him, because I liked someone else. And, of course, not just anyone else, but North...which I couldn't do because well, that just wasn't allowed. Until I said something to correct the situation, Everett got to look all cool while I came off as a loser. Emma must've been trying to read my face for a reaction, because she said, "Then why would he say that?"

Not ready to deal with the situation, I changed the subject abruptly, "What's the other thing?"

If it was possible, Emma looked even more uncomfortable. I held up my hands and said, "I promise, I will not kill the messenger."

"Really?"

"Honestly."

"You know the color guard instructor?"

I didn't want to let on just how well I knew, or what exactly I thought of Denise, so I said calmly, "Yes, I know who she is."

"Apparently, well, the rumor is that..."

"Yes?"

"She's threatened to talk to Ms. Jenkins about bringing Marti or Jenny in to help conduct the band."

My classmates hadn't come near the band since their departure in the spring and I wanted to keep it that way. Over the summer, the Parktown marching band had become well and truly mine. I responded as such, "That's ridiculous!"

Emma looked visibly relieved at my reaction and said, "Yeah, that's pretty much what I thought."

"I'll handle it – and thanks for letting me know."

Watching Emma's retreating figure, I realized how completely naïve I was. I also knew I didn't want to back down. If this was how Denise was going to play, well, I wasn't going to give up without a fight, and I sure as hell wasn't going to let someone else come in and share the title with me. Win or lose, this was my band and no one else's.

At the moment, there wasn't much I could actually do, other than express my frustration, and since I was pretty sure Jude was way over his limit of ventitude, I decided it was time to bring in Heather. Having neglected our friendship for my obsession with the band, I hadn't been as good a friend as I could in the season so far.

"What would you do?" I asked, after telling her the drama that was my life over pizza at our favorite local place.

She quirked a blonde eyebrow at me and said, "There's a few more things I need to know. First of all, do you like North?"

"Why does it always come back to that?!" I yelled, disturbing a few of the patrons in the restaurant. I still failed to see how my liking our instructor had anything to do with how well my band was going to do this season, but I guess I was wrong.

"I'll take that as a yes," she replied.

"Sorry, it just seems to be a big deal and I don't get it."

"Rigby, you're the drum major — not just some random person in the band. What you do and say matters to a lot of people. Who you like also matters. I know it shouldn't, but it does."

"I guess I didn't realize that when I auditioned. Silly me that I thought I would lead the band to victory — that all my hard work and determination would pay off. What was I thinking?"

Heather took a sip of her soda, chewed on the straw for a bit and then said, "I hate to tell you, but that's the way it is. You can accept things, or whine about how unfair life is, but being the former drumline girl you are, I know you're going to get over it. Now, I'm sure you didn't plan on the complications from North at the beginning of the season."

"Definitely not."

"...but that issue aside, you also have to understand Everett's pride took a major blow, not only once, when you avoided kissing him, but again when you admitted you liked another guy. What did you expect him to do?"

"Get over himself and be my friend?"

"Really?"

"Do you think I would've told him about North if I thought he was going to go spreading made up rumors about me?"

Heather was quiet a moment before she answered honestly, "Yeah, I'm glad the biggest thing I have to worry about right now is nailing the 32nd note run at the end of the closer."

Although I was being selfish with the conversation, I asked, "Honestly, what would you do if you were me?"

"I think you have to kind of be above it all."

"Do you think that's going to help?"

"Do you have another option?"

"The truth?" I asked in a small voice.

"No offense, Rig, but I don't know if your band can handle the truth."

"Thank you, Mr. Sorkin."

"Seriously, I think you should just sit back and see how things play out. From what you've told me and what I've observed, it sounds like at least part of the band is loyal to you. Give them time to win over everyone else. I think they liked it when the band was functioning as a whole."

"A band divided against itself cannot stand!"

"Rig, you need to lay off the history class and focus on making yourself happy. I think everyone will respond to that."

"And how do I do that exactly? You make it sound so easy."

"You don't know what makes you happy?" She signed and finished the crust she had been nibbling on.

"Go back to the basics. Everything else will work out from there."

"You're right."

"Of course I am!"

As we laughed and said our goodbyes, Heather's words stuck with me on the way home. What did make me happy? Band. Yes. Being around North? That too. Why wasn't there a way to have both? Didn't I deserve to be happy? It was my senior year after all.

This week's football game was away, which was just as well, because I didn't want to be embarrassed publicly at our home stadium. Until I could figure out a way to reunify the band, I was more than happy to play to other audiences besides our own. I knew most people probably wouldn't care and couldn't tell the difference in our playing, but I could and did.

I'm not sure how I managed it, but again, I was the last on the buses. As I scanned the seats, it appeared the only available seat was with North. I slid in next to him, making sure to keep some space between us. The week had not done anything to improve our situation, but for some reason, I was still hopeful of some final reconciliation. However, judging by the stoic North sitting next to me, that future didn't seem to be in my future. I slowly pulled on my headphones, scrolling through my music until I found something appropriately melancholy and wondered for the first time in the season wondered if my life wouldn't have been a lot easier if I wouldn't have auditioned for drum major at all. If I would've stayed in the drumline and with Everett, we could've had fun for my senior year instead of the current mess I was calling life. I had given up a spot in the best section of the band to become a lonely section of one – what had I been thinking?

Without meaning to, I sighed deeply.

North tapped my shoulder and mouthed the words, "Everything okay?"

"Sure," I said back to him, meaning completely the opposite.

North looked like he didn't believe me, but let me get back to my music, then tapped me again, and although I could see something like anger flashing in his eyes, there was also concern as he asked, "Does it have to do with Everett?"

This time I took off my headphones and responded, "Does what have to do with Everett?"

"I heard."

I instantly rolled my eyes and replied, "Of course you did."

"Look, Rig, if that was your reason for us to have some space – you could've just told me. I think I could've handled it."

Without thinking my comment through, I quipped, "Yeah, that's what you would see."

"What's that supposed to mean?"

"I don't know, maybe you should go tell Denise about it." I was being an immature brat, but I didn't care.

He crossed his arms and growled back at me, "What the hell is that supposed to mean?"

"You figure it out."

He sighed and fiddled with the clipboard in his hands, "Look, Rigby, I'm not going to lie to you – this week has sucked."

"You can say that again."

"But until you're willing to come clean about whatever it is you have going on, then well..."

"What?"

North looked out the window, past the landscape passing by and asked, "You want to why I broke up with Denise?"

"She cheated on you?"

If he knew I knew, he kept the surprise to himself. He finally responded, "That's the funny thing. It's not even that."

"Then what was it?"

"She lied about cheating. She lied about a lot of things. I told myself that the next relationship I was in, there would be no lies."

As my mind reeled from the phrase 'next relationship,' North's phone went off and interrupted our conversation. He looked apologetic as he picked up the phone and said, "Hi, Ms. Jenkins? Sure, we can talk about tonight."

By the time they finished their call, we were at the high school...and the conversation was a memory, but not one I was likely to forget.

Chapter 14: A Parktown Miracle

Nothing else came of North's and I's almost conversation. Furthermore, I was too scared to approach him to see what he meant by 'next relationship.' What if he was talking about me? Then again, what if I had read the situation completely wrong and he wasn't talking about me? I came to the conclusion there wasn't much to do but sit back and wait. Wait for everyone to work out whatever animosity and anger they had towards me. Waiting wasn't easy, but I managed, and then, without much effort or thought, it was competition time. The funny thing about a marching season is that at the beginning, it feels like there is so much time, and then suddenly, there's no time and a performance is upon you. Via the usual social media, I had heard various rumors regarding Harrison-Benavidez and what their response to us would be, but honestly, I had bigger things to worry about. Like, my life. It had gone from 'Yay, I'm so proud of myself because I made drum major and am being all kinds of responsible,' to 'I'm pretty sure sections in my band flat out don't like me, and there's nothing I can do about it.'

So, we went to our first competition. Me, Everett, Denise, North, and our giant bus full of awkwardness. Realistically, I knew we were probably going to place where we always did – the bottom three, the laughingstock, the 'why did you even bother to put on a uniform today?' placement. Other schools went to competitions knowing 'at least they couldn't do as bad as Parktown.'

But then, a small miracle happened. Starting with our warm up, we actually sounded, well, good. Sections tuned and harmonized in a way they never had previously. Hoping my luck was holding, I stepped outside the tuning circle and listened for the drumline. Delighted, I heard some of the cleanest sounds they had ever produced. I glanced across to the color guard, running through their routine and saw nothing but clean catches and no drops. They even looked in unison. Things were coming together like I always knew was possible and, as we took the field for competition, magic happened on the field. From the moment I gave my salute – crisp, precise and perfect – to the moment I brought my hands down at the end of the closer, I was in total disbelief at the sound and show we had just performed.

As we walked off the field, everyone seemed too scared to talk about what had happened on the field. Not wanting to jinx our band, I made small talk with the group, but made sure not to mention anything about how good I thought we did. As much as I wanted to get into an involved conversation with North about the show, the most I could muster was to ask simply, "Seven?"

He gave me a smile and said, "Seven and a half."

This was by far the highest number we had ever achieved and even just the number was high praise. I walked away, trying to keep the smile on my face to a minimum. We had our picture taken and then returned to where the busses and equipment truck was waiting to put away our instruments. As one of the first bands to perform, we basically had the rest of the day ahead of us, and Ms. Jenkins let everyone change back to their regular clothes. The section leaders and I would have to change back later in the day. As much as I wanted to sit with the drumline, a glare from Everett changed my opinion. Heather and the rest of the flute section once again welcomed me and together we watched our competition. Although small, there was a tiny bit of optimism in me – the hope we might actually hear the words 'Parktown high school' called out over the loudspeaker during the awards session.

Checking my phone, I realized it was time for our band leadership to meet up. With wishes of good luck from the collected woodwinds, I went to our buses to put on my drum majorette uniform. Once back in our beloved polyester, Ms. Jenkins had us gather in a section to watch the last group of bands perform. The only thing to do now was wait. On autopilot, I sat myself with Ms. Jenkins, North, and a growly looking Denise. Well, she could get over herself. It's not like I was going to make out with North right in front of our band director. Anyways, it was a secret pleasure of mine to sit with people who understood what they were watching and pick shows apart. Sure, it was immature and shallow, but I wanted to think we had a small chance.

When Harrison-Benavidez took the field, my heart started thundering in my chest. As the perennial favorite, they always got the crowd, warmed up by this point and at least ten times the number we had performed for earlier in the day, involved with their show. They had improved from their last performance, but I could tell the three drum majors were still a bit off from each other. Their error wasn't obvious, but it was there. As the audience clapped enthusiastically, I looked to North for support and, without me even having to say something; he nodded, confirming my opinion. I smiled to myself.

No matter what happened (or didn't happen) between us we would always have marching band as our common ground, and that had to count for something.

"Any reason you were talking to her?" Denise asked from North's other side as HBHS cleared the field and the exhibition band set up.

"None of your business."

Although I wanted to know why he was talking to 'her' as well, Denise's words helped me learn a small lesson. I didn't want to come off petty and jealous like she was. North didn't 'belong' to anyone, not her, and certainly not me. Too nervous about the results and too annoyed by our color guard Instructor to keep still any longer, I abruptly stood up, straightened my uniform and said, "I'd better go line up with everyone."

Ms. Jenkins nodded and said, "Remember Rigby, whatever the judges do or say, I know we did a great job today and you should be very proud of yourself."

North made direct eye contact with me, giving my system a definite jolt of adrenaline, and said with a small smile, "Just remember, this is supposed to be fun."

Denise, of course, did not say anything.

Walking down to the field with my little group, I wanted to call Everett out for the stupid rumor he had started, but decided it wasn't worth the effort. If he wanted to be immature and not accept my whole moving on and trying to be friends scenario, then what was I going to do? I couldn't force him to change his mind, and I couldn't compel myself to have feelings for him again. What I could do, however, was treat him like the great drumline captain he was. I said simply, "Good show today."

"Thanks."

Recalling an inside joke and particularly memorable (and regrettable) performance from our freshman year on the Line, I added, "Better than the Mulan fiasco of our freshman year."

Try as he might, he could not help but grin.

Naturally, when we lined up on the field, who should we get placed next to? None other than my best friends and ardent supporters, the DM's from HB. Although we were all supposed to be at attention, their sarcastic commentary started as soon as the announcer started listing the sponsors. I couldn't turn my head, and neither could they, but their voices carried across our small space.

"Caught your 'performance' earlier…"

"Did we? I didn't think we ever got here that early."

"They were on the field when we came in."

"Oh, I guess I didn't hear them – they must not have been loud enough."

Because the drum majors lined up at the front of their respective bands, and they were speaking in low tones, I knew their sections couldn't hear what they were saying, and neither could mine. As much as I wanted to dig back, to argue, I knew that part of me had earned their harsh comments. At the same time, I had pride and I knew I had conducted a great show. I couldn't help myself from blurting out, "We'll see what the judges say."

It seemed like they had been waiting for me to speak, eager to jump on me.

"You think the judges are going to place some hick-town, no-name nothing band ahead of us? You've got to be kidding."

The announcer's voice boomed across the stadium, "We will now announce the scores. With respect to all bands, please hold applause until the end."

We got straight Superiors – a first for us.

HBHS got straight Superiors – nothing new for them.

Then the captions wee announced and I wasn't surprised when our school wasn't called for any of the categories. I would admit I was a little disappointed, however, it was still possible to have a technically and musically challenging show and not win captions. We weren't totally ruled out...

"In the category of drum major..."

I instantly perked up, hope springing eternal. Although I was a one woman show, I still had a very demanding score to conduct.

"In third place, Mountain Creek HS." My heart dropped as I watched a pair of drum majors go to collect their trophy.

Hence, you can imagine my disbelief when I heard the announcer call out, "In second place, Parktown HS."

It might have been the first time our name had ever been called in relation to an award. I was too stunned to move, and felt Emma and Everett's hands on my back, pushing me forward. I saw our little section of the stands going absolutely crazy. They were making enough noise for a band three times their size and the enthusiasm was infectious. I dropped my drumline serious face and adopted a big smile, shaking the judge's hands, and posing for a picture. Striding back with my trophy, I wondered who would be in first.

"In first place, South Washington HS."

I sat stunned for a minute, as did my neighbors to the left. Harrison-Benavidez hadn't won! They didn't place in my category! As petty as it might be, my second place finish made their loss that much sweeter. There wasn't time for me to say anything, but I don't think I needed to. Being as obvious as I could be, I put my little trophy out in front of our band. Never in my wildest dreams did I picture this happening. For me, our improvement was enough, that we had pride in our organization, that we had come so far. But somehow, this moment had made all the crap I had gone through over the summer and throughout the season totally worth it.

I wondered what North was thinking. Was he proud of me?

In a haze of the unexpected win, I must've spaced out for a little while, because suddenly the announcement for Sweepstakes was upon us. Reaching the end of the Top 10, the announcer hesitated a moment before saying, "As we have an even tie for second place, we will not give out a third place award. Would band representatives from Harrison-Benavidez and Parktown High Schools please step forward to collect their awards for second place?"

Ms. Jenkins approached me after the awards ceremony, and said, "First of all, congratulations!"

She wrapped her arms around me in an awkward hug, but I smiled. Ms. J. wasn't so much with the obvious emotions, but I could tell she was proud. She continued, "And second of all, great news, Rig, we've been invited to an invitational."

"Huh?"

"Apparently, the top three bands from this competition are invited to a major band competition in two weeks."

My heart all but stopped. There was only one contest on the marching band calendar that mattered. I asked, "The Stoll Invitational?"

She nodded.

Nearly overcome with emotion, the wheels in my brain turned slowly, and I asked, "How did we not know about this?"

Ms. Jenkins grinned sheepishly and said, "We never placed in the top three before."

We had already come so much further than I had ever dreamed. Sure, I allowed myself to think we would not embarrass ourselves on the field, but to be invited to the next level of competition? We didn't have fancy technicians or instructors for every section. We didn't have the newest equipment or uniforms. We definitely didn't have the biggest band. But for our size, I knew, and it seemed others agreed, we had an awesome sound.

My band director continued, "Keep it a secret until we're back at the school – I'll call everyone to attention and let them know back in the band room."

"Yes, ma'am."

As Ms. J walked away in the direction to some of the band parents, I was literally bursting with happiness and pride. So, I couldn't help my reaction when the first person I saw was North. It felt so natural to throw myself at him and he responded, sweeping me up in a big hug. As he settled me back to the ground, I noticed he didn't let go, that his arms were still gathered around me, holding me close. I didn't want to release my arms around his neck, because the embrace felt so right. To be held by him – to share this moment, which we had both been working towards – this is what I would remember from my senior year. Daring to look up, there was an almost moment, similar to the one that had happened so many weeks ago in my driveway. I held my breath, but in the middle of a crowded competition was hardly the place to, well, I wasn't sure what was going to happen next, but whatever I dreamed of would definitely be inappropriate. Unfortunately, I was almost certain that anyone walking by would pick up on our major sparks, so I slowly took a step back, making eye contact with him and trying my best to let him know, well, at the very minimum, I wanted to keep hugging him.

With a smile matching my own, he asked, "Why are you so excited?"

I clasped my drum major trophy to my chest and answered, "We're going to the Stoll Invitational!"

Although I'm fairly certain North had no idea what I was talking about, he responded, "Wow, that's fantastic news!"

It was then Heather found me and squealed, "I'm so proud of you!!"

North smiled at me and headed towards the rest of the band. I watched him walk away, and for once felt something approaching normalcy. If only we could get Denise out of the picture, there might be a chance at a real relationship. Turning my attention back to my friend, I asked, "Really?"

"Yeah, you were so intimidating out there. It was like, of all the drum majors, you were the most drum major-y."

"Uhh, thanks?"

"Don't mention it."

My friend joined my arm in hers and together we joined the rest of the Parktown band.

Chapter 15: Every Little Thing She Does is Magic

The ride back to the school that night was a comfortable one. I couldn't wait to listen to the judges' tapes, and had brought along a tape player just so I could hear what they had to say. Of course, when I had packed my bag in the morning, I had no idea I would be listening to an award winning performance. As soon as roll had been called, I pulled on my noise-cancelling headphones and clicked the 'play' button. I was not disappointed. Saving the drum major tape for last, the sounds from earlier in the evening came across from varying perspectives on the field and the judges' box. The notes for me were few, and the compliments many. Maybe it was because our performance was earlier in the day and the judges were still feeling generous, but I smiled the entire time I was listening. It's like the collective judging staff had been waiting for a Cinderella story like the Parktown Pirates to come along.

I could've also been smiling because I was sitting next to my favorite instructor – an equally happy and smiling North.

Back at Parktown, everyone brought their instruments into the school in a great mood. If this evening had been last season, we would've been joking about our many mistakes, laughing at our failures and abysmal placement, but tonight, there was something extra. Even though the hour was late, Ms. Jenkins called us all to attention.

I tried to keep my face impassive as she announced, "I've got some great news, kids. Based on our performance tonight, we've been invited to a major competition in two weeks. I was talking to some of the other band directors, and I want you all to know what an honor it is we'll be going. I think this is just the first step in the first of many things the Parktown band can be proud of. Get a good rest this weekend, and we'll be ready to practice on Monday."

With a big layer of icing on their already loaded cake, my marching Pirates trickled out into the cool night, with all sorts of plans to celebrate circulating the halls of the school. As a section of one, it occurred to me I had taken for granted the time and closeness I'd had with the drumline. Even though part of me was desperate to see North, tonight felt like a time to be with my band. And, honestly, if Denise wanted to think she had a chance with North, well, she could go ahead and try her luck. I didn't need someone to validate the chemistry which had been radiating between North and I. Like with the band today, I think I just needed to wait for the right time. There was no magic wand that could make things happen, except for when they were supposed to, and nothing could change that. Tonight was definitely proof of that fact.

Some of my friends on the bass line casually mentioned where they were going – the usual drumline hangout – and while I thanked them, I was a bit on the fence about going. On the way out to the car, I called Jude – hoping I wasn't interrupting whatever nocturnal activity he was up to. Having accidentally walked in on more awkward situations than I wanted to, I knew calling or texting was usually the most reliable way to get in touch with my brother.

He answered on the second ring, "Hey Sis, how'd you do tonight?"

"Not too shabby, I won second place and the band did too!"

"Wow, good stuff. You must be proud."

"Yeah, I am."

"Anything else going on?"

I'd had enough awkward conversations with my brother to know he must be with someone, so, I asked point blank, "Should I go out with the Line or should I try and find North?"

"What do you want to do?"

"Both," I answered honestly.

"Has North given you any indication he wants to see you?"

I thought back to our happy bus ride and almost moment, and even though my instructor hadn't asked me specifically, I honestly felt like anything could happen tonight.

"Umm...don't you always tell me you like it when girls ask you out?"

"Rig, you don't need my approval, I may have mentioned this once or twice, but do whatever – or whoever – you want."

"Thanks for the sage advice, O Brother Mine."

"Anytime."

I was still no closer to a decision, but before I could make up my mind, I saw Denise had beaten me to North. I took her interference as a sign, and headed towards my car. Joining the Line at our local pizza place, I settled back and watched everyone interacting. The flirtation, the inside jokes, the need to attention – the camaraderie. The behavior made me realize while I was obviously still one of them, in some ways I had moved past much of what had brought us together. I wasn't massively more mature, or looking down on everyone, more that I had made my peace with high school already. Being here proved it. I already had a trunk of memories with my section and the members – past and present, to last me a very long time. I knew there was always a place for me in the percussion section, but tonight, my place was supposed to be somewhere else.

As I would forever cherish my time as a member of the Parktown drumline, tonight was time to make some future memories.

Hating the drama of goodbyes with the entire section, I waited for a Robert, the section comedian, to begin telling a story and casually pushed back from the counter. Leaving some money on the table, I faked going to the bathroom and snuck out of the restaurant. I thought I had made away without anyway noticing when I heard someone cough loudly behind me.

"And just where are we off to this evening, Miss Sullivan?"

"Nowhere, Ev." I stopped, and hesitated, about to put my keys in the door, vaguely bittersweet he still knew me so well.

"I..."

I heard his voice catch, and figured he had earned at least a little more of my time. We had dated for three years, after all. I turned and answered, "Yes?"

"I'm sorry for giving you such a hard time with North."

Everett sounded like he meant what he was saying. His being with me along with his recent flirtation with a certain junior saxophonist made me optimistic that actually being friends during our senior season together was a possibility.

"That's okay." At the end of the day, whatever crap Everett had dished out to me seemed retribution for me breaking up with him so many months ago. I was ready to move on, and glad he was too. Finally.

"And, well, I thought you should know, I'm proud of the way things turned out tonight."

I immediately turned the compliment back to him and said, "You had a big part in how—"

"Shh. It was you, Rigby – you were the one who turned the band around, and I'm only mad at myself for trying to stand in your way."

"Thanks, Ev. It means a lot. I'll bet we have an actual shot at winning next weekend."

"You really think so?"

"Everett Herman Wallace – we went up against Harrison-Benavidez tonight and won. Right now, I think anything is possible..." My voice trailed off, and I think he and I both knew what I was referring to.

"It's just..."

"I know."

And I knew he knew. Neither of us needed to say the words. Everett would forever be my first love – and I his, but now it was time to see what the next romantic phase in my life would be. Having Everett's 'blessing' as it was, wasn't necessary, but I'm glad I had it.

"Good night, Ev."

"Take care of yourself, Rigby."

Blaring my favorite tunes, singing at the top of my lungs, I drove around Parktown, keeping my eyes peeled for a certain beat up Indian motorcycle, but as much as I wanted to will North into existence in front of me, I couldn't find him. As badly as I needed to see him, I resisted texting him. To me, nothing could wreck the magic of the day and I decided that if North wanted to find me and we were supposed to be together that night, he knew where I lived.

Pulling into my driveway, I suddenly realized it was very early in the morning. My parents had long since tried to keep strict curfews on us – Jude's paramour activities made them not even try and fight the losing battle. As long as we both kept our grades up, we were allowed late nights and a high degree of trust. I didn't usually take advantage of their leniency, but tonight seemed extra special and I wasn't ready to go upstairs to bed.

Although it was cold out, I took my time walking up the path to the side door.

"Psst..."

I wasn't surprised or scared to hear a voice. First of all, Parktown wasn't that kind of place, and second of all, with Jude being a teenage boy, I had come home to everything from a variety of pranks from the cross country team to a semi-clad brother locked out of the house – surprised when some neighborhood girlfriend's parents had come home early.

Who I didn't expect it to be was North.

"Rigby."

"You must be freezing."

Yeah, I was a winning conversationalist pointing out the obvious and all, but still, it was a cold night in late October – he had to be cold. Who knew how long he had been waiting?

"You're kind of right."

"Come inside?"

"Are you sure that's okay?"

I glanced at my phone and saw the LCD screen light up – 3:00AM, and answered, "I'm pretty sure Mom and Dad Sullivan are asleep – plus, we've got a finished basement, so they won't be able to hear us."

I cringed inwardly at how overtly sexual my statement sounded, but still didn't ask for an answer, and was happy when he followed me silently into the quiet house.

Turning on the lights, I took a seat on one of the couches, and he took a seat across from me, warming himself up. We both removed our jackets, and I thought about what I wanted to say. Cooped up to him so many times on a bus, in the stands, during practice, he should've been the most easy person in the world to talk to, but at that exact moment, I couldn't come up with anything to say. Until finally it occurred to me there was still one big unanswered question. I asked bluntly, "So, why did you tell her about our ride?"

There was no question who 'she' was, or what I was referring to. North ran a hand over his dark hair and answered, "I don't know, I guess I thought, well, hoped she would get the point."

"And what point is that?"

"I thought if I told her about our ride she would see there wasn't room for her anymore..."

"Because?"

"Because I liked you."

While I was floored by this information, part of me was frustrated by how everything – the season so far and all of its hassles could've been changed if he had just admitted this simple fact to her weeks ago. At the same time, I felt lighter than ever, and wanted to immediately put the nasty business of Denise behind us. She was in the past, and whatever happened between them, well, it didn't matter. I was his future.

"Really?"

"Really," he answered and scooted closer. I tried to calm my nerves, which were flying about the room. I had pictured this moment since I met him, and now – it was actually happening! He leaned in carefully, slowly, drawing the moment out... I closed my eyes and held my breath, leaning in to meet him.

BRAAAPPP!!!!!

A giant belch sounded at the top of the stairs, followed by some loud footsteps clattering down to the basement. Sighing heavily, North gently pressed his forehead to mine and whispered, "I'm going to kill your brother."

Those words were among was the most romantic thing I had ever heard.

We had enough time to move apart, but Jude, no stranger to this business, started smiling broadly as he walked across the room, outwardly comfortable in his years old sweatpants and a cross country shirt from his freshman year.

"Thought you were in bed, sis."

"Obviously, I'm not, Jude," I growled back.

"Oh, hi North – how's it going?"

"Just fine, thanks."

Rather than taking the obvious hint we would rather be left alone, Jude sat right next to me and cuddled me close. I shoved him away, and realized he might be getting retribution for any of the many, many (many!) times I pulled this sort of thing between him and his dates. After he had hit his stride during the fall semester of our junior year, I had given up even trying to bother with the never ending stream of girls in our basement. If I wanted to go downstairs and play Rock Band, well, no one was going to stop me. Still, how could I communicate to my brother this was more than any of the flings he had been involved with? That North could be the real thing?

North stood up and keeping eye contact with me said apologetically, "Well, I'd better go."

"I'll walk you out," I said instantly.

"Nah, I parked down the street, and I don't want my bike to wake up your parents. Plus, it's cold out. I'll call you tomorrow, er, later today."

His comment wasn't what I wanted to hear, but waiting would have to do. My eyes were growing tired anyway. I walked with him as far as the stairwell, away from Jude, who was already lost in his gaming.

North looked at me – hungrily – but settled for a gentle kiss on the top of my head, and murmured, "Soon."

I sighed happily, and went and sank down on the couch – tucking myself up and pulling a worn fleece throw over me. After shooting a quick glare at my brother who was happily blasting things on screen, I passed out, perfectly content with the entire day – one of the best I could remember.

My slumber was broken by a buzzing.

I blinked sleepily and saw not much time had passed. Jude was passed out in the chair across from me, sleepily snoring away. I rolled my eyes and looked for the source of the buzzing. Surprisingly, it was my phone.

Even better – it was a text from North.

Chapter 16: Homecoming

I woke up disoriented. I had been having the most wonderful dream...where North and I were...well, anyway, I didn't want to wake up. Snuggling under the soft fleece blanket, I tried to recapture those images, but failed, and woke up to find myself alone in the family basement. Had last night actually happened? Had North been waiting for me? Did he almost kiss me? Had we won a spot at the Stoll Invitational? I looked around and not surprisingly, my good for nothing brother was nowhere to be found. He had always had the ability to go on almost no sleep and still get up for his morning run. Suddenly, it hit me – I had evidence of the night before! I grabbed for my phone, which I must have passed out using and scrolled through the conversation Jude and I'd had. Smiling to myself, I blushed as I read over the texts, wondering what had come over me. The last message, 'sweet dreams' would keep me smiling for the rest of the day. I stretched and then went upstairs, unprepared for the amount of sunshine that hit me.

"Morning, Rigby," my dad said from behind the newspaper. "Glad you decided to join us."

"Congratulations, by the way," my mom added and flopped down the local newspaper at my place at the table. Apparently, given how big Parktown was, our placement at the competition was enough to be front page news – complete with my picture on the cover. Considering the majority of Sullivan journalistic moments had been because of Jude – his amazing ability to run and many scholastic achievements, this article was a big deal to me. My heart swelled with pride, this was the kind of recognition my band could be proud of. "It says here you've been invited to some sort of special competition in a few weeks."

"It does?" I asked, grabbing a bagel and lathering it with cream cheese.

My mom looked across at my dad and said, "We'd love to watch you."

The thing I liked most about my parents is they gave Jude and me our space. They weren't helicopters or involved in each and every single element of our lives. If they could, they would catch a practice and usually attended the Friday night games (even if they left right after halftime) and even though they weren't moving pit equipment or on uniform duty I knew they supported my marching efforts. I thought back to how much they had interacted with North this season. So far, it had been a casual introduction (my mom had noted particularly 'what a dish' the instructor was). With how North and I's relationship was evolving, I wasn't sure how much more I wanted them interacting. Still, my parents were smart and if I told them not to attend, they would definitely know something was up.

"Sounds great," I mumbled with enthusiasm and stuffed my face with bagel, hoping we would change the conversation.

"We'll even bring Jude," my Dad said.

"Even better," I said.

As predicted, Monday's sectionals buzzed with anticipation. Even without my involvement, it seemed over the weekend the entire band had done their homework. Every section was clamoring about how they could improve parts of the show. Their suggestions ranged from 'suicides' for the trombones to some sort of crazy flag toss for the color guard. North, Ms. Jenkins and I sorted through the ideas, decided which to try out and keep what worked. With a limited amount of time left in the season, the three of us also decided we would put all of our collective resources into the invitational. There were other competitions in the area, but with our limited budget, we would need everything to get across the state. Our decision considerably upped the pressure we were putting on the group, but I personally liked the idea of go big or go home. Even if we came in dead last, at least the underclassmen were getting exposure to what real competition would feel like. The improvements were grueling, time consuming, and I felt like my arms were going to fall out of their sockets from the amount of conducting I was doing – but the hard work was awesome and there was nowhere else I would rather be. We worked out every step, every comment the judges left us – we talked about every note, every phrase, and every set of the show.

At the same time, I settled into a comfortable place with North. We both seemed to recognize whatever we had – and it was definitely something special – that we would just have a wait a few weeks more until we could be open with whatever our relationship was going to develop into. It went without saying we couldn't express whatever feelings had been brought to the surface the night of the competition. And somehow, waiting made the potential that much more exciting. Rather than communicate things publicly, we had continued furiously texting each other. Although I couldn't share our relationship with anyone, just knowing things were moving forward was enough for me. Whenever I saw Denise fawn all over North during practice, I had to hide a smug smile, knowing we would discuss her useless actions later.

On top of perfecting the show and getting comfortable with North, we also had to dedicate our class time and one practice to learning the Homecoming arrangement, due Friday night. Everyone seemed unenthused with the theme 'A Night in Paradise' and I was grateful Ms. Jenkins who basically rushed us through what we would need to do and didn't care at all that no one would memorize the music. She was fine with the entire band reading the music on the field. For my part, the conducting was a snap and with all that was going on in my life, I was grateful for something easy.

Additionally, in a first I could ever remember, Jude was without someone for the big dance. He didn't seem to mind and on our way to school on Friday morning, he turned down the volume (it was my week to control the music and with things going right with North, it was a lot of upbeat and sappy songs of the romantical persuasion) and asked, "Y'know, since it's our senior year and everything, why don't we go together tomorrow?"

"Wouldn't that be totally lame? You're my brother." Even with invitations to go with unattached friends in various sections, I was planning on skipping the whole debacle, I considered his request and answered, "Besides, don't you have someone to go with?"

"Nah, I just want to go and pick up the pieces when the inevitable Homecoming drama goes down. You know, I haven't worked the whole 'knight-in-shining-armor' angle in awhile."

I rolled my eyes and answered, "You're gross."

"Nah, I'm just honest."

I already had a dress I had picked up over the summer when my mom was feeling generous and at least with Jude I was sure to have a good time. I hesitated a moment longer before saying, "Okay."

"Excellent."

"But you have to get me a corsage – and not a cheap one."

"Sure."

The thing was, for most people it would be lame if they went with a sibling, but being twins, and kind of popular twins at that, we could pull it off. Furthermore, I didn't particularly care what anyone at Parktown thought. Warming up to the idea, I asked, "Who are we going with? Your friends or mine."

"Just leave it up to me."

I didn't trust his tone of voice, so I said, "Fine, but our evening better not involve getting drunk with your track friends."

"Trust me, sis, it's going to be a night to remember."

The conversation with Jude was a memory later that day. Although I think we had collectively holding our breath, the band's performance after Friday night's game was a large improvement. We were able to talk the school officials into letting us go though the show after the game and I was delighted to see a number of friends, fans and classmates stayed on to watch and cheer us on. The overall improvement was amazing to witness.

The next evening was a decidedly unexpected senior year moment at the Sullivan household. In an unprecedented first, we were all home. I took most of the afternoon getting ready – kind of ridiculous really, given my date was just going to be Jude, but I had fun being a girl. I tried out a few different hairstyles, before deciding on a sleek blowout. As we came down the stairs together, my parents actually got a little teary eyed when they realized this was one of the last moments like this they would have before we moved on to college. They made us recreate a number of childhood pictures and we all had a good laugh.

My dad sent us off by saying, "Don't have her out too late, son!"

We drove away giggling. The way things were looking, I was leaning strongly towards majoring in music education at the big state school and Jude was deciding which of the athletic or scholastic scholarships he would accept. It was sad to think we would be separated, but as much as we were, you know, born at the same time and everything, my parents had done an excellent job of raising us as independent kids. Frowning slightly, I realized with Parktown being kind of small, I thought I knew all the restaurants. When Jude turned down an unfamiliar road, I looked at him hesitantly, and questioned, "Where are we going?"

"Some place original. Trust me, I think you'll like it."

By the time we pulled into an apartment complex, I had to wonder what was going on. More so when Jude chuckled and said, "Oh, come on, sis, you cannot be that naïve."

It wasn't until I saw a very familiar motorcycle that I figured out what was going on. For some reason, I had never thought about where North lived. I mean, sure, I knew he had to live somewhere, and somewhere was in town, but this was different.

To cover my surprise, I asked, "Is he, um, expecting us?"

Jude smiled, pulled up, parked the car, and responded, "I'll see you in about two hours and then we'll crash the dance for the last couple of songs. Sound good?" "Where are you going to go?"

"Don't worry about me – just have fun. He's in 402."

Walking up the stairs of the apartments, I felt a little ridiculous in my ensemble, but also pleased North would be able to see the prettified version of me, rather than the constantly sweaty, hair pulled back, t-shirt and track pants I seemed to favor every day of practice. Taking a deep breath, I knocked on the door – which immediately opened to reveal a very handsomely dressed North. He wasn't in a suit like Jude, but he was wearing a navy button down shirt and dark jeans. The collar was unbuttoned enough I glimpsed something I had never seen before – distinctly permanent ink peeked out the top. My eyebrows raised and I made a mental note to ask him about the tattoo later.

North's smile matched my own and he asked, "Are you surprised?"

"What? Yes..." And I wasn't just talking about how I had ended up here.

I looked around the apartment, and while it definitely screamed 'bachelor pad,' I could tell it had North's interests in mind. There was a ragged couch and used entertainment center, but also some cool art and posters on the wall. He had a number of vintage jazz posters and records albums framed which somehow worked with various snapshots of himself in various uniforms. There was a small hallway, and I assumed it led to a combination bedroom with bathroom. "Nice place," I finally commented.

"Yeah, it's okay."

From what I knew, North was spending the days he wasn't with us travelling back and forth to the classes he was attending to finish his degree. Apparently, he was some sort of brain and had started college way ahead with credits. Student teaching would come in the spring. He continued, "So, um, I'm not very good at cooking or anything, so I hope you don't mind macaroni and cheese..."

Since he gave me the world's cutest smile to go with his request, there was nothing I could do but nod in agreement.

"Sit down and make yourself comfortable, and by the way, since I haven't told you yet, you look stunning," he called over his shoulder.

As he walked over to the kitchen, I took a deep breath and not freak out because I was a high school senior sitting in someone's college apartment. Okay, I'm not that naïve or anything – I had dated Everett for the better part of three years, but still. Whether I had actually voiced my opinion yet, I knew Denise and she seemed so much older than me. Then I forced myself to realize this time next year, I could have a place of my own. As a freshman in college, for the first time in my eighteen years, I would be on my own and making all kinds of individual decisions. So, really, what was the point of being nervous?

"Open my computer and pick out some music," North added.

I did, and wasn't surprised to see a very eclectic and large music collection appear in his iTunes. Resisting the urge to do any sort of snooping, I smiled at the choice of his background screen – our group band picture, taken earlier in the year. Opening the familiar icon, I scrolled through and found an eclectic collection of composers, rap artists, and a lot of stuff I wouldn't have expected.

"Katy Perry? Really?" I giggled.

"I'm sure you can guess who added her."

She had to come up at some point. Denise had been strangely quiet over the past week, and I couldn't figure her action, or rather inaction, out. Had she finally accepted North wasn't into her anymore? Or was she lurking and waiting for us to mess up? Technically, my being here could put a number of things in jeopardy (most importantly North's job and my reputation), but besides Jude, there was no one who knew I was here. Pushing my concerns aside, I settled on Jack Johnson's latest and sat back awkwardly in my dress on the well broken in couch. Even though I didn't want to ruin my Homecoming evening talking about exes, this was the only place we could talk freely, so I asked, "Has she talked to you this week?"

"Not really. Not that I mind."

He walked over with two steaming bowls of cheesy macaroni. Hey – I wasn't complaining. Everett had had his own ways of being romantic and I knew sometimes you had to look a little deeper to see smaller gestures probably meant something more.

Changing the subject, I asked, "So, what's up with your tattoo?"

Grinning, he pulled open his shirt collar so I could see the entire thing. The squiggles appeared to be a stanza of music complete with notes. I squinted and tried to recognize the tune, but couldn't come up with if the phrase sounded familiar or not. On my confused look, he said, "It's something I wrote. The notes are part of a larger composition." "Very cool," I responded. "I'd like to hear it some time." "Definitely."

Chatting about our favorite topic – the show – we finished our dinner and I volunteered to clean up to which North was happy to let me do. He looked on as I struck an interesting pose in the kitchen – glammed out in my dress and Homecoming makeup with plastic gloves on my hands while I scrubbed the dishes. I had worked all afternoon on my manicure and wasn't about to wreck my efforts. Finishing up the last dish, I noted North leaning on the doorway, and realized he had never looked sexier.

"All finished," I said, peeling the gloves off slowly, and, my voice full of meaning, asked, "What should we do now?"

We locked eyes and, there was a brief moment, a hesitation, a heartbeat...

Then, the months of staying apart had finally reached their crescendo and I wasn't surprised when we met somewhere between the refrigerator and the dishwasher, our lips and tongues clashing. Somehow I ended up on the counter with my legs wrapped around North, and what followed was as an intense a make out session as I had ever experienced. It wasn't until I heard Jude knocking on the door I realized how much time had passed. Trying to pull myself together and not look so obvious about what we had been up to, while also trying to get my breathing back to normal, I couldn't stop smiling. All the waiting had completely been worth it.

"Have fun tonight," North said quietly.

"I already did…" I whispered, sliding off the counter, and heading towards the front door.

Chapter 17: Looking Ahead

Stepping out of North's place in a bit of a daze, I stumbled into our car. Jude looked strangely at me, and taking in my messed up hair, plumped up lips, and general disarray, did what any brother would do. Holding up his hand, he said playfully, "High five for getting some, sis!"

Embarrassed, I knew he would not let up until I met his palm, so I slapped his hand and we drove away.

"So, what next?"

"It's complicated."

Jude rolled his eyes and said, "Sometimes, I wonder how we came out of the same womb."

"You're gross."

"You're changing the subject."

I looked over at my brother and said, "What do you want me to say? That I'm hopelessly in love with the band's instructor? Fine, I am. That everything is going to work out fine? It's not. That North is like one of the random girls you hook up with? It's different. That this is some sort of magic world where we can actually be together? Because it's not!"

Jude sighed loudly and replied tersely, "Would you stop thinking about what everyone wants? Stop thinking about what I want, what he wants, what our parents want. What do you want?"

Put in my place, I crossed my arms and sulked, feeling a bit sorry for myself. Tapping his hands on the steering wheel, Jude replied, "Come on, sis, you deserve to be happy. Now, let go see what this dance is all about."

Once inside, intent on getting official evidence of the night, I herded Jude over to where the photographer was set up.

"Just think what your future niece or nephew will say!" I said, while being silly with the scenery.

"They will probably hope they are adopted," Jude replied through smiling and clenched teeth.

"Next!" shouted the photo guy, clearly glad to rid of us.

We walked further into our darkened gym, made beautiful by thousands of fairy lights, and Jude quickly scouted the dance floor. With a particularly devilish smile on his face, he said, "I see my damsel in distress now. Let me know when you want to leave."

Rolling my eyes, I watched him walk away and went in search of some of the Parktown marching band kids. I was all set to do the group grove thing, when the strains of a familiar Van Morrison came over the speakers. Without meaning to, I looked across the room and spotted Everett looking in my direction – we had matching smiles on our faces. Surprisingly, he had escorted young Emma to the dance tonight, and I honestly hoped they worked out as a permanent couple. Although she was a bit hyper, Everett could be a bit slow sometimes, so maybe they could balance each other out. As the notes filtered across the gym, I knew this had traditionally been 'our' song and it would always feel weird to dance with anyone else but him.

My ex-boyfriend made his way over and, with hands stuffed in his suit pockets, asked, "Want to?"

His proposal wasn't the most romantic request I had ever received, but I knew the question came from a good place. I nodded and wrapped my arms around Everett's familiar shoulders. His presence felt comfortable, but I hoped he realized the spark we once shared was gone. I might as well have been dancing with Jude.

We swayed slowly and he said, "Don't read into what I'm saying, but you look great tonight."

I privately wondered if my glow had anything to do with I had done earlier with North. Half the fun was having the secret. On the way into the gym, classmates had made a point to mention how wonderful I looked.

"Yeah?" I finally responded.

"Yeah." He was quiet a moment before he said, "You know what?"

"What's that?"

"I know I'm not supposed to bring up the past or whatever, but this seems forever ago from where we were last year."

I leaned my head gently on his shoulder and thought back to our junior year. Twelve months ago, I thought we would be together forever. A year ago I had no idea I would be drum major, that I would meet North, or that a lot of things would turn out the way they did.

"I know."

"We'll always be friends, won't we, Rig?"

"Yes, Mount Everett, we will."

He was quiet a moment longer, before he asked, "Speaking of which, what are you doing after the dance?"

I gazed across the other couples swaying in time to the music and saw my brother with some cute blonde wrapped securely around him and answered, "Well, as predicted, certainly not going home with my brother. Why?"

"Jake's having most of the Line over if you want to crash."

As tempted as I was to go directly back to North's apartment, I realized showing up unannounced and without protection probably wasn't the best decision. A Parktown drumline sleepover probably wasn't the most mature way to spend my evening, but I realized given it was my senior season, I might regret not spending the time with old friends. I answered, "That would be awesome. Do I need to bring anything?"

"Nah – I think we're just going to order pizza."

"Cool, well, I need to go home and change first and then I'll be there."

"Bring your camera."

I laughed, remembering the bizarre and crazy photos and plethora of inside jokes that had come from last year's event.

"Will do."

The song came to an end and, dipping me as he usually did, Everett said, "See you later."

"Definitely."

I went to find Jude. Thankfully, he and the blonde had come up for air. Tapping him on the shoulder, I said, "Hey, bro." Not bothering asking for an introduction to his 'date,' I asked, "Ready to split?"

Jude reverted to some sort of mental conversation with his date I was oblivious to, and replied, "I'm going to catch a ride home here with Tiffany. Here's the keys to Yaya."

"Thanks."

After rushing home and changing into sweats and a t-shirt, I drove a few neighborhoods down and pulled near the curb near Jake's house. Recognizing the other cars in the driveway, I knew almost everyone was already inside, but couldn't force myself out of the car. Putting my keys away, I pulled out my battered cell phone and looked at the screen. Should I text North? Would he want to hear from me? Would that be too needy? Not that messing around had to mean anything in particular, but in my world, I assumed it brought our relationship to a more serious level and yet I wasn't sure how to approach the subject. I typed a number of different opening statements on my keypad, but erased all of them. Hence, my surprise when my phone lit up with a text message from North.

>> *How was the dance?*

I smiled, glad for the opening volley and immediately typed:

>> *Lonely without you.*
>> *So is my apartment.*

Well, that answered the question about how he was feeling about me. Not wanting to dwell on the part of the evening without him, I typed back.

>> *What can I say? Your mac and cheese was inspiring.*
>> *I think it had everything to do with your dress.*

As the conversation carried on frantically from there, needless to say, I was red faced and grateful for the cool night air as I walked into the house. Everett gave me a once over as I walked in, but didn't say anything. Trying to put my conversation with North behind me, I threw myself into hanging out with my former section. We played video games, ate junk food, and decorated one of the freshmen with the contents of my make up bag after he passed out at 1AM. Given the intense practice schedule, we all passed out relatively soon after.

I woke up the next morning to the smell of pancakes, the sound of our freshman year show blaring from the television and a big smile on my face.

Sitting up from my sleeping bag, I was surprisingly lucid and suddenly had this life altering thought occur.

How had I not realized it before?

For the longest time I had been wondering 'what I was going to do with the rest of my life.' Jude, smart guy that he was, of course, had his plans all already figured out. He didn't deny his materialistic streak, but also knew he wanted to make a difference. He was going to fast track himself for an MBA, then try on the world of consulting (of course, he also had some major travel plans and a few business ideas built in). I, on the other hand, hadn't been able to articulate what it was I was going to study. Jude had already received his early acceptance to Harvard, while I was still waiting to hear back from some state programs and community colleges closer to home. The appearance of North had made the university up the road a more attractive one, but I knew it was an emotionally charged decision and ridiculous to go somewhere just because my boyfriend was (or whatever our relationship was). However, what North was studying suddenly made a lot of sense. Every time I stepped on the podium, I had the best feeling ever. So, why couldn't I direct on a permanent basis? I had the basics, and college was supposed to be about getting skills for the real world, wasn't it?

And just like that, in an instant, my future laid out before me. Who knew? Maybe in a couple of years I would be leading a college marching band? Ideas started pouring into my head. I couldn't wait to share the good news with North.

Rubbing the sleep from my eyes, I bounded into the kitchen grinning from ear to ear. Everett caught my expression and asked, "Have a good dream there, Rig?"

After a few inappropriate comments from the bass line, I replied, "I think I know what I want to do with my life."

My announcement was a bit too early in the morning for such deep and meaningful comments, so I wasn't surprised when, in response, Jake asked, "Pancake or bacon?"

Back at school on Monday, with one week to go until the invitational, we worked. North called in a few favors and brought in friends, talented musicians, and various other professionals to help us tweak our show. Note by note, step by step, side by side, we broke down the performance from the very beginning and built it back up. With confidence and skills I didn't know our little band had, we steadily grew as a group. Our transitions were perfect, the notes had never been more crisp or in tune – in short, the show we had started with at band camp had finally reached the level it was intended to be at. As I was always curious on the subject of Denise, I couldn't help but notice our external helpers' reaction to her. A few were friendly, but I got the overwhelming impression that most seemed to keep their distance.

Unfortunately, although I didn't have time to worry, from the background, Denise lurked. I felt relieved knowing she didn't know what had happened between me and North over the weekend, but I wasn't entirely sure she had completely let him go. We were so close to finishing the season and I felt if we could make it past the invitational, I would be able to breathe a sigh of relief.

On top of everything else, while I had been outwardly projecting confidence – and believed in every section, I still found it difficult to trust myself. It seemed like I was still waiting for some judge to call me out and telling me to quit faking – to get back in the drumline where I belonged.

I did well to hide my lack of confidence from North, but didn't have the same luck with my twin. Jude noticed something was off with me. We were on our way to school the Friday before our big competition and I was nervous.

"Yo."

"What's up?"

"You're doing it again."

I had a tendency to conduct at the weirdest times. I had been directing so much in the past few weeks that leading imaginary bands was pretty much my default motor skill.

"Something bothering you?"

"No. Why?"

"Look, I know you have to be all rock star hard core drum major around the band, but this is just me – your brother."

"Okay, fine." I tucked my hands under my legs and said, "The thing is, I'm kind of nervous."

"You don't say?"

"This is not the time for sarcasm."

"I know, but isn't it a little late for that particular emotion?"

"No. Maybe. I don't know."

"Rig, everyone gets nervous. I get butterflies before every race. Stupid thoughts come to me – have I tied my shoes? What if I forget the course?"

"Really?"

He shrugged and answered, "It's not every time, but I know those thoughts are ridiculous. You're going what everyone goes through."

I turned down the volume on the radio and said, "Okay, so, Mr. I Have The Answer to Everything, what would you tell me to do?"

"Research."

"That's all?"

"That's pretty much what everything comes down to."

"Seriously?"

"Yup. Do you homework. Whatever it takes."

I knew there was footage of the other bands out there, but had been avoiding the images and videos. I didn't want to see how good they were, how good they had always been, how we didn't compare. But maybe, I might see that we were good too. I knew my rational side was begging me to ask North about my skills as a conductor, but I just didn't think I had it in me if he told me I sucked. As mature as I thought I was, I didn't want to resent the guy I was dating.

I was quiet and Jude said, "Promise me you will, Rig."

"Okay."

"How are things going with South?" he asked playfully, lightening the mood. Since Homecoming, Jude had promised to keep North and I's relationship hidden from the parental units. I'd covered for him countless times and he was great at supporting us.

"Couldn't be better," I gushed. Jude was the only person I could talk to about my new boyfriend. I didn't trust anyone else to keep the mouth shut about things.

Jude made a right hand turn onto the street Parktown was located and asked, "So, graduation's kind of a long way off, isn't it?"

"We haven't talked about things specifically, but he'll be off the county payroll at the end of the season. We only need to keep things cool until then."

"Do you think you can handle that? I know boys have needs, how about the ladies?"

"Unlike you, brother dear, I know how to keep my hands to myself. Anyway, North is worth it."

"I'm glad things are working out for you two. You deserve some play."

I rolled my eyes and asked, "Seriously, how do you think Mom and Dad will take it when they tell them?"

"Not sure."

"Not sure – good or bad?"

"As the alleged older twin, you've always been more mature, maybe they'll be okay with it."

"North wants me to tell them."

Jude's eyebrows raised and he replied, "I don't think honesty is too bad a policy here."

"I'm okay with telling them – just as soon as the competitive season is over."

"So, any time after tomorrow?"

"More or less."

The following morning, with a flurry of secret pal gifts, a spotless inspection, and, as I had been doing since the beginning of the season, sitting while Adelaide carefully braided my hair into a beautifully intricate coif, the Parktown marching band prepared for the biggest competition our program had ever faced. As we packed the buses and equipment truck, I was surprised to see a bunch of parents (mine, with Jude in tow, included) and a few teachers on site to see us off. Last season, the crowd had been the usual band (helicopter) parents, with us inevitably getting a late start, because someone (usually a section leader) had 'run into traffic.' Ms. Jenkins would just kind of go along with things. From there, we would be too late for a proper warm up and would go out on the field, unprepared and rushed.

Today, however, Ms. J (cleaned up in a crisp black pant suit and appropriate school colored tie) had everyone, sans instruments, line up in a concert arc and stand at attention. The parents hung at the back and listened.

She clapped her hands together and stated, "Well, gang, I never thought we would get here. I've been teaching at this school for over 10 years and I'm speechless. I have never been prouder of a group. I know where you came from and I can't believe you got here. No matter what happens today, win or lose, I hope you look back at this season and know you can accomplish anything."

As Ms. Jenkins continued to wax sentimental, I thought about my audition, about how I thought we were going to be lost without Marti, how when all this started, I didn't even know North existed.

"So let's go and make Parktown proud!"

Knowing I would get to make my speech before we took the field for competition, I was happy to remain quiet and let our band director have the initial push to get everyone excited. We all cheered and broke attention. North came up to me as we approached the buses and I said, "You know what's funny?"

"What's that?"

"If you would've asked me a year ago if I could've imagined any of this, I probably would've laughed in your face."

North paused a moment, and I could tell he was thinking back to where he was, before we met, before we even knew the other existed. Finally, he answered, "I'm glad things worked out the way they did."

I realized for all the choices I made, if I hadn't made drum major, North and I wouldn't have spent so much time together. Fate sure had a funny way of working out.

Ms. Jenkins came up to us, and said, "You know what the best part of all this is?"

"What's that?" I asked.

"This," she pointed to our little Parktown marching band who were diligently double checking the components of their uniforms and that everyone was accounted for. She continued, "This is permanent. I can see it on everyone's faces. They like winning – they like the feeling. And so do I."

I was tempted to ask why she hadn't done anything about this earlier, but realized it was the wrong time and maybe not my place to ask. Better understanding North's own particular and complicated back story, maybe Ms. Jenkins had something (or someone) who had been holding her back all this time. None of that mattered now. Today was going to be our day. We were going to make an impression on people and they would remember our little band.

Denise joined us. As she stood next to us, I wondered if she realized her plan had failed. Her attempt to get North back, to insert herself back into his life had come up short and while I would admit she had finally whipped the color guard into shape, I would also agree that it took her long enough to get there.

Eying the pretty color guard instructor, I noticed my brother saunter up to me and whisper, "Care to introduce me, sis?"

Denise took care of things for me. She asked bluntly, "Rigby, who is this?"

I couldn't tell if she was more excited there was another guy in my life that wasn't North, or that she might have a genuine (ick) interest in my brother. Even though I was glad for his support, I half wished Jude hadn't shown up today. Knowing he would most likely rather be anywhere else made his presence that much more thoughtful.

"Denise, this is my twin, Jude."

"Hey Jude," she said, as if she was the first person to ever come up with that particular joke. I sighed loudly and Jude indulged her, while they laughed together and I went to collect my uniform and talk to the section leaders.

Chapter 18: Ups and Downs

Like some long crescendo, my nerves started building on the bus. Before now, there wasn't anything to get worried about, nothing to be anxious over. We had nothing to lose and everything to gain as a band, so I hadn't been nervous. But now… What would happen if we got to the Invitational and fell flat? If we placed last? Would the whole band blame me for forcing them to be here? Was this whole season an exercise in my ego?

Apparently in tune with my inner meltdowns, after checking to see no one was looking, North gently took my hand from my mouth, as I had been chowing down on my fingernails since we got on the bus.

"Sorry," I said.

"What are you so worried about any way? Do I need to remind you that just being on this bus is a sign of how successful this season is?"

Rather than answer his questions, I blurted out, "Am I a good drum major?"

As a chaperone neared our seat, he put my hand down and asked, "Where is all this coming from?"

"Look, I know all the other sections have had help and advice and someone to see them through, but this week I realized I never really have."

He paused and then answered, "Don't you think I would've helped you if you needed it?"

"Umm..."

"Rigby, believe me, you have nothing to worry about."

"Are you sure?"

"Are you fishing?"

"Maybe..."

"You're a natural. When you conduct, it's obvious you were meant to be up on the podium."

"Really?"

"Really."

With all of our preparations for the show, I hadn't yet told North about my dreams to become a band director, and wondered if this the right time to bring up the subject. Usually, when it came to life altering decisions and plans, Jude was the default person I bounced stuff off of. However, this choice seemed like something I wanted to talk to with North first. In the past week, there hadn't been any time for meaningful conversations – I had barely been enough energy for me to get my school assignments done before I crashed exhausted into bed every night.

And yet...

With my last moments of consciousness every night I had time to dream about my future. I wanted to find a band program like Parktown and start at the beginning. I wanted to build things up from nothing. I wanted to start a dynasty. And sometimes, I could picture North with me. Together we would find this amazing school and work as a team. There could be generations of kids we could help. Maybe we would even have our own kids in the program. A drummer. A jazz musician – it didn't matter. Ours would be a household of life and laughter and music. Maybe I was crazy – but the potential of my future made me smile.

"You know, you've given me an idea. I'm going to talk to everyone, see what they're nervous about, okay?" said North, getting out of his seat and moving towards the aisle.

"You are a great instructor. We're – I'm – lucky to have you as part of our group," I told him warmly, realizing I probably didn't tell him enough. We had more or less taken North for granted since he had arrived and help change everything.

He gave me one of his best smiles and said, "I know."

While he made his way through the bus, I pulled on my headphones and listened to the show once more, closing my eyes and visualizing our award winning performance.

When we pulled up to the competition, I knew from the first look at the campus we were entirely out of our league. There were more marching bands than I had ever seen. Although it was still early in the day, there, in every combination of colors imaginable were uniforms and flags and equipment. North looked out the window and commented, "I guess we'll have to show them what Parktown can do."

I gulped, and then permanently adopted my game face. I knew the band would be looking to me and I wanted to exude confidence. I was the first to step off the bus, and was glad for the warm sunshine. The temperatures were cool, but the sun above made it tolerable. All in all, the conditions added up to a perfect day to march. As the rest of the band trailed off the bus behind me, I knew we were one of the first bands competing, which did not make it easier for my group. From experience, I guessed most judges would leave room for higher scores later in the day, for the bigger programs – the ones with more of everything – more people, money and bigger sections. It was an uphill battle, but I wasn't going to make excuses for us. If we were going to win, our accomplishment should be on merit. I hoped the judges would keep an open mind, and let our show speak for itself.

Given our performance time, we had to immediately go to the warm up and staging area. Ms. Jenkins and North had gone to collect our information packet, leaving me alone with the band parents, the section leaders, and Denise, who had disappeared somewhere. As I ducked into a restroom to finish pulling together my uniform, I let the band leadership warm up with their respective sections for a few minutes before I called everyone back together. Not sure what was taking so long with my director and instructor and more than ready to get my own warm up underway, I called everyone to attention.

"Champions!" I shouted out.

The particular piece was my favorite chorale we used for tuning. The arrangement also never failed to bring goosebumps to my arms. Today was no different. The piece ended in perfect harmony, and at the same time the drumline ended their warm ups.

Ms. Jenkins and North must have joined us sometime during the warm up, because when I brought my arms down, they were standing behind me. Deciding this was my moment, I cleared my throat and suddenly emotional, said, "Guys, I know I probably wasn't the easiest person to work with earlier in the season. In fact, the whole season. I pushed you and made you do laps. I made you sweat and cry and do the show..."

"ONE MORE TIME!" everyone shouted at the same at the same time, laughing.

"I promise!" I finished my part of the joke, then said, "Look how in sync we are! Seriously, when I sat in front of Ms. Jenkins and made my case to be your drum major – I warned her it wasn't going to be easy." My voice hitched and I struggled to get through the final emotional words, "But then you all went and surprised me – and even though we've had our differences, you have made this easily the best season I could ever hope for. We've put Parktown on the marching map – and for all the good reasons. I know we talk about pride and spirit, but I hope you know how much I feel that for each of you. Thank you for making my senior year such a memorable one."

Afraid I would completely lose it and ruin my make up, I clapped my hands together and bowed to the group. Ms. Jenkins put her hand on my shoulder, looked proudly at us, and said, "Okay guys, five minutes to go, everyone line up in two rows – Pit, you need to come with me."

I took my place at the front of our group, and was all ready to go when I realized I still had my cell phone jammed in my skirt. I looked around frantically, and spotted Jude talking to Denise. Although I was annoyed at him, especially after he had heard my repeated diatribes against her all season, I knew he didn't take most females seriously, so I decided to things go. After all, she wasn't talking to North, so that fact was something positive worth noting. I had enough going on today than worrying about my brother chatting up yet another girl. Even if she annoyed me, if Denise wanted to fall to his charms, I certainly wasn't going to stand in their way.

My parents were busy talking to some of the other band moms and dads who had joined us and North was going over last minute instructions and tuning with the low brass. Fortunately, at that moment, Denise decided to act more like the instructor she was hired to be and less like every other girl at my school. As she made her way to the color guard, I approached my brother and asked, "Can you hold this for me?"

He quickly pocketed the device and replied, "Sure thing. I guess you don't want to get a call while you're up on the podium."

"Really? You think?" I answered sarcastically, then asked, "Jude?"

"Yes, Rig?"

"You do realize you're talking to the Denise I've been bitching about for months, right?"

"Yup."

"Just checking."

We stood still, me in my polyester drum majorette finery, Jude in jeans and his varsity cross country jacket and I said, "She will never come to our basement, understood?"

"You got it. Trust me on this. Now, go on, you've got a show to do."

As nervous as I was, the moment my booted heel stepped onto the soft green grass, all was forgotten. I was here and I was ready to win. The announcer listed the section leaders, then North and Ms. Jenkins's name, before my own and I felt a swell of pride. We fell into opening set, fanning out and taking over the field. I stood on the fifty-yard line in front of the band.

"Drum major, is your band ready to take the field for competition?" The announcer's voice echoed across the stadium.

Confidently, I snapped off my salute in crisp perfection, then stoically walked over and climbed the director podium. My heart was calm, my hands were steady and I clapped in tempo, and then called the band to attention, "Band – ten hut!"

"HUT!" The answer came roaring back to me.

I gazed out over the field and saw the opening set wasn't precisely where I wanted it to be and called out, "Dress center dress!"

The band shifted accordingly, and I was content. We were now ready to start the show. It always seemed like an out of body experience when I got in the zone of conducting, and I could feel my brain shift to the music.

Softly, I said, "Mark time hut..."

As I conducted the beats, I heard Everett and the rest of the Line dut softly from the field, with my firm down beat of 'one,' the show moved to a roaring start. I moved my arms passionately, going through the pages of music of the score, until I reached the closer. With goosebumps running down my arms, I brought my hands down to put an end to the triumphant show. I bowed to the judge box and lifted my hands to show my appreciation to the band. Whatever score we were given, I knew on every level our performance was perfect. Other bands may have more difficult runs and drill, but for what we had been given, we did the best we could.

Everett tapped notes on his snare drum and I led the band off the field. As soon as we were in the designated recovery area, the group erupted into simultaneous cheers and high fives. We had done it! We had pulled off the best show Parktown high school had ever seen. There were hugs and exclamations and everything I had dreamed of early in the season.

Ms. Jenkins held her hands up and said, "Great job out there, gang! I could not be prouder of all of you. Now, as you are aware, there is some time until the awards are passed out tonight. First, we're going to go back to the buses and change. After the dinner break, we'll get together at a section in the stands and all sit together for the awards. At that time, our section leaders will need to change back into their uniforms for the awards ceremony. Until then, I encourage you to all sit and support as many bands as you can. I also remind everyone to stay in groups. You'll need to stay on campus and call any of the parents if anything comes up. Finally, please remember that today you are all ambassadors of Parktown and should act accordingly. Don't forget, school rules apply here too."

After we posed for the group picture (equal levels of serious and crazy), the band quickly dispersed and I walked slowly with North and Ms. Jenkins back towards the equipment truck. Unable to hold my emotions in any longer, I asked, "Seriously, how did we do? As good as I thought?"

North nodded and answered, "After I left you, I ran up and got as close as I could to the press box to see and hear the whole show. I'm not lying or being partial when I say the performance was amazing. I give it an 8.5."

The highest score yet! Grumbling to myself about how long we would have to wait, but knowing I could get to spend the whole day openly with North (in professional capacity as drum major and instructor, of course), I didn't mind so much. Being mindful of my elaborate hairstyle, I carefully changed out of my uniform, zipped it up, and joined North who was waiting for me.

"Where do you want to go first?"

"Actually, I'm kind of starving," I admitted, after we dropped my uniform on the bus. I had been too nervous to eat anything that morning and given all the adrenaline and energy I had expended, I was more than ready to eat.

On our way to the food stands, we ran into my parents. They had, of course, met much earlier in the season, but, mostly due to my own arrangements, hadn't interacted much past the initial run through of the show at the conclusion of band camp. Although I do not think they loved me any less, my Mom and Dad weren't the parents who came and watched each and every one of my rehearsals (nor did they go to Jude's every practice or meet). They came to the occasional football game, but since I was so busy being drum major, I never got a chance to see them more than to usually say hello and borrow some money. My parents had liked Everett just fine, but the relationship was something that had developed naturally, and he was a classmate of mine. I wasn't sure how to announce I was involved with North. Fortunately, North was much less socially awkward than I was and took the first step.

"Hi there, you must be Rigby's parents. I think we met earlier in the season."

They all shook hands and my Mom said, "Such a great job out there today, honey."

Never one to take compliments gracefully, I kind of shuffled around and mumbled, "Thanks, Mom."

She tucked her arm around me and pulled me close, "No really, it was truly something. You looked so intense. I'm sure you guys will win tonight."

Was this the point where I told everyone my future plans? I knew my parents were proud of my brother and me in different ways, but how would they react to my announcement? Did they want a band director for a daughter? There had been increasing pressure over the fall for me to 'get serious' about what I wanted to do next year. Should I tell everyone as a group?

I took a deep breath and said, "Really? Because that brings up something I want to tell you and Dad."

North looked in alarm at me, and I gently shook my head.

My Dad asked, "What is it?"

"Well..."

Just then, I saw Ms. Jenkins, with an expression I had never seen on her face before. It wasn't a good thing. Then I noticed she was holding something in her hand...my phone.

And then my heart plummeted into my stomach – I had kept a number of very revealing messages from North on my cell from the night of Homecoming.

Chapter 19: They Can't Handle the Truth!

A million thoughts raced through my brain for a way out of this crazy situation. The fact my parents were present certainly wasn't helping the matter. Was it only moments ago my life had been completely sane and normal? I suddenly dreamed of grabbing North's hand and running away, of denying it was my phone Ms. Jenkins was holding. In addition to being terrified, another and completely different emotion washed over me — I was royally pissed off. There was only one possibility of who could be behind this, and it certainly wasn't my brother.

"What is the meaning of this?" Ms. Jenkins demanded. For someone who rarely raised her voice, she sounded very angry.

My parents looked at me, and I looked at North. Finally, I answered innocently, "What specifically are you referring to?"

"These...these text messages!" she sputtered.

"Oh, those."

My parents, who were genuinely lenient people, started to look wary. I didn't know and couldn't gauge what their responses would be. The texts weren't exactly PG material, and taken out of context, I could see why Ms. Jenkins was almost speechless. However, I also knew my Dad was three years older than my Mom, which was about how far apart North and I were. Also in my favor, Jude wasn't exactly a saint – I had witnessed him getting away with far worse stuff for the past two years and was fairly certain the parental units weren't going to pick now to start using a double standard. Anyway, if it was this time next year and I was bringing home a 'nice young man' from college, where would the problem be?

My Mom began to tap her foot impatiently, which was never a good sign. It was her equivalent of yelling, so I was on edge. She asked, "What is he talking about?"

I wondered who would be in more trouble. Would Ms. Jenkins fire North on the spot? Would my parents ever trust me again? Given this interaction with North, could they ever like him? Was there some way I could take the blame for all of this? After all, it was my fault for keeping the texts, and my colossal mistake for trusting my phone when Denise (who was suspiciously nowhere to be found) was around.

Ms. Jenkins looked at North and asked crisply, "Can you explain yourself?"

North stared her straight in the face and replied, "Can we please have this conversation somewhere private?"

I looked pleadingly at my band director, whose face softened for a moment and she then nodded tersely.

"I'll explain – I promise," I told my parents, as we walked away.

We marched silently through the campus until we found a deserted bench and Ms. Jenkins exploded, "I don't know what to do with you two!"

"Do you even want to hear our side of things?" I asked. Instead of getting irrational or upset, I hoped to show Ms. Jenkins how mature I was by not getting emotional or shouting (or tracking down Denise and hitting her squarely over the head with my drum major baton like I wanted to do).

"No. Yes. Why couldn't you wait until after the season? Or after graduation? There are rules I have to follow."

"Can I ask how you got this information?" North asked, crossing his arms. Ms. Jenkins looked uncomfortable. Yes, what we had done wasn't technically legal, but when it came down to it, we were consenting adults.

"It was Denise, wasn't it?" I chimed in, wondering if she had thought her actions through. Didn't she realize she could potentially be wrecking North's entire future as a music educator? How could she be so petty? At this point, I wished she would've tried some creative blackmailing versus the situation we were in now.

"It doesn't matter or how where this information was received, I have to do something about it."

"Would it help you to know that nothing, of, um, a personal nature has occurred on school grounds or during my work hours?" North questioned.

Ms. Jenkins's shoulders slumped.

"Who else knows about this?" I pleaded and continued "Denise? If she's the only one, then what is the problem? I'm 18 – this is all legal, I'm a consenting adult. It's not like he's a teacher or something."

I wanted also to add it wasn't as if we had been carrying on some sort of torrid love affair all semester, we were basically talking about one night of making out! There was no way that could count.

My band director shook her head and said, "He is paid by the county – through the school board. As far as we're legally concerned, he's an employee."

"Still, you're not going to be able to prove anything," I said, and continued, "We're both going to deny whatever you say, and you don't have any real evidence.

Anyone could have sent those messages – North could report his phone was stolen."

Just then, North looked at me and gently took my hand, surprising both me and Ms. Jenkins. He said, "Look, I realize this is a grey area. I know on paper it is classified as 'wrong,' but, and you have to believe me, I know this," he pointed to both of us, "is right. What Rigby and I have, well, neither of us planned it, and we spent an entire season trying to deny it was there. Can you just let us be happy? Can you look the other way? After today, I'm no longer employed by the county. What difference does one day make?"

Smiling, I gripped North's hand and said to my band director, "Before you say anything, please just think about your answer. Can you remember what it was like to be young and in love? No one got hurt here. And you may think I'm naïve and immature, but I would be happy to sign anything that said I won't come back and make things difficult for the county. As far as I'm concerned, what North and I have is a private matter between the two of us."

"I'll think about it." Ms. Jenkins moved to walk away, then handed me my phone and said, "I believe this is yours."

With the faint strains of the next band performing behind us, we were left in relative silence. The discovery of my phone had forced a lot of things forward. I was genuinely touched with North's impassioned plea and hoped his words were enough to sway Ms. Jenkins.

"I'm sorry," North admitted.

"Why?"

"This is my fault."

"How?"

"I should've… I could've controlled myself. I'm supposed to be the older one here."

I smiled, touched at his misguided gallantry, and said, "We tried that, remember? It didn't work. I think the more important thing right now is to worry about your future."

"Do you think she'll go through with things? That she'll make 'us' public?"

I considered. Even from the difficult conversation we had just had, from what I could tell, Ms. Jenkins was basically a decent person. I said, "At the worst, she'll probably come out with some weird form of punishment for the two of us."

"I hope you're right."

"And if I'm not?"

"We'll have to deal with whatever happens."

And somehow, I didn't feel as bad. If it was the both of us, well, I could handle things. I sat down on the bench next to North and leaned on his shoulder. I asked, "Did you mean what you said?"

He nodded, and I smiled, then I put my head in my hands and looked at the ground, my face rapidly becoming red.

"What's wrong?" North asked.

"You probably think I'm completely obsessive for even keeping those messages."

He laughed and sheepishly pulled out his own phone, then silently opened it and scrolled to his saved messages, passing it across so I could see the evidence. Mine were all there. I started laughing. My reaction was the only thing that seemed normal in this unlikely situation.

"Why?"

I answered honestly, "It's just the overall state of the universe right now. So many things could have been different today, but they weren't. If this happened tomorrow..."

"You know, we always were going to have to face the consequences at some point."

"I know, but, you know what?"

"What's that?"

"I think the good kind of outweighs the bad in this scenario."

North squeezed my hand and said, "Agreed."

We were quiet for a few minutes. I knew I needed to regain my composure over the crazy that had just occurred. Finally, I asked, "So, what do we do about her?"

"There is nothing we can do today."

"I know," I grumbled, genuinely upset I would have to delay my retribution.

"I think we'll have to avoid her, because if I see her...well, I'm not sure I'll be able to control what happens next."

"And my parents?"

"Are you ready to deal with them?"

"You know I don't want to hide you or us, right?"

"Yes."

"But at the same time, I don't think this is the venue to bring up the fact that we're dating, agreed?"

"I understand."

I leaned into North's shoulder and said, "If it makes you feel any better, we have Jude's full support."

"It kind of does."

"Have you told any of your friends about me?" The question was out before I realized it. With all of the help North had brought in over the past week, I had privately wondered if any of them knew about North and I's relationship. Would they think what any outsider see – that North was pervy and creepy? Or could they look past our age differences and be happy for him to enter into a new relationship?

"Sort of."

"Sort of, who?" I asked, suddenly curious.

"My friend Bronwyn." I wasn't inherently jealous, but I also didn't want there to be a ton of other ladies in North's life. He smiled at my obvious response and continued, "She's in the music education program and happily dating someone else. I promise."

"What does she think?"

"She just wants me to be happy. She knows me well enough to know I'm not taking advantage of you."

"Does she know Denise?"

"Peripherally. We were all in the same band, but not all the sections overlap all the time."

"So Denise is the reason you didn't march this season?" I asked, voicing a concern I had always wondered about. North seemed to enjoy marching so much and with all the time he was giving us, there was no way he would be able to balance both college band and instructing Parktown.

"Yes."

I thought of how much he would have to have been hurt to give up something he so clearly loved. As weird as things had been with Everett, I never once thought about giving up the band.

"Do you regret it?" I asked.

"Sometimes, but then I realize I would have missed out on this season with you and how far everyone has come."

"I hope it's been worth it."

He squeezed my hand and said, "Believe me, it has."

Even with the amount of chaos that was probably going to rain down on us, I felt better than I had all season. Looking at our linked hands, I said, "Ready to go back to everything?"

"If we must."

Reluctantly dropping each other's hand, we walked back to the stands, both nervous and unsure of how the day would play out. I was frustrated and angry and unsure where to direct my feelings, which was rare for me. Having had to share things my entire life with Jude, I didn't get too worked up over the little things that seemed to irritate everyone else. Today, however, I realized Denise had been the one thing standing between me and a perfect season. From her entrance at the start of the season to her stunt today, she basically made the world a less fun place and for that, I couldn't forgive her.

I let countless calls and texts from friends, Jude and my parents go unanswered. North and I found a relatively out of the way corner to watch the shows and camped out for most of the day. Ms. Jenkins found us later, right before the dinner break. On what could've been one of the best days of my life, I was having an absolutely terrible time. I was hyper critical of all the bands that performed, picking them apart and being cattier than I had ever been previously. I was distracted and thought I saw Denise everywhere I looked. I couldn't control myself – waiting for the other shoe to drop was taking all the energy I had.

Spotting us, Ms. Jenkins said, "You two. Let's go."

We followed my band director to where we had our original conversation. Ms. Jenkins paced back and forth. She finally said, "I've been thinking about this all day. I don't know who to punish, or how it will help, quite honestly, I don't even know if there is a lesson to be learned here. As much as I want to discipline you, I also realize that how I received this information must play into the equation."

"So, what will you do?" I asked.

"I will tell you in a moment. Don't ask me to change my mind. If you do, well, I'll have to go through the appropriate channels for this, understood?"

We both nodded, and I held my breath.

"First, North, for you and Denise, I think it's entirely fair that neither of you will be asked back next season, nor can I give you any letter of recommendation for your work. I will not speak out against you, but I will not say anything good. I will only confirm that you worked a season for me. I think, and hope, however, that your work this season will stand out. Can you handle these terms?"

North sighed and answered, "Yes."

Ms. Jenkins turned to face me and said, "Now, Rigby, it pains me what I'm about to tell you. However, I can't let what you did go unpunished. As you mentioned, if you are mature enough to enter into this relationship, then you are mature enough to handle the consequences. As much as I could put the blame entirely on North, given the limited texts I read, I know you were an active participant in circumventing the rules."

I continued to hold my breath as Ms. Jenkins continued, "You will not represent the band tonight at the awards ceremony. You will not join the rest of the group in the stands. You will sit on the bus and think about what you've done this season."

Glad I was already sitting on the bench, I felt the air quickly leave my lungs. I couldn't control the two tears that quickly leaked out and had to choke back a sob.

Not join the band? The band that I had made? The only chance I had as a senior to see us win? To flash our win in the face of my friends at Harrison-Benavidez? To stand proudly in my uniform as the leader? Ever since Ms. Jenkins had posted my name as drum major, I had dreamt of this day, barely believing it was possible. And here my moment was, so close – only to be ripped away. As pathetic as it was, I couldn't find my voice to argue. At the end of the day, I was a student. As unfair as the decision was, Ms. Jenkins was my teacher, and in this situation, seemed to have all the power.

On my behalf, North practically growled his response, "No way! That's completely unacceptable!"

"What do you mean?"

"Think about what you're doing, Nancy. Look, I don't care if you punish me, I don't care I won't get a recommendation, but you're taking something away from Rigby she can never get back – this is her senior year, and quite honestly, the only one that's really counted with Parktown. I know what we did is wrong, but I'm willing to take all of the punishment. If you need to go public about this, I'll tell people whatever you want to hear."

"My decision is final!" And with that statement she stomped away, leaving us in silence once again.

Chapter 20: A New Band for the Night

I sat in shock, still numb from the punishment that had been handed down to me. Random thoughts started bouncing around my head. First of all, I never got in trouble – like never – that was usually Jude's department. This instantly made me think I shouldn't even be in trouble. What about my rights to privacy? Didn't that count for anything? And more importantly, why did Ms. Jenkins, the biggest pushover I had ever known, suddenly choose today to stand up for herself? Why couldn't she wait until tomorrow to make herself into someone with a spine? Her overreaction seemed a bit out of character. Basically, why, after everything I had been through this season, did this have to happen to me now? I was well over character building and anything else the world wanted to throw at me. This was the one remaining hour of my senior season that mattered and not at all how I planned things.

"I guess I should go to the bus." The words sounded hollow and empty and I couldn't actually bring myself to get up. To get up would be to admit defeat, and I wasn't ready to go there just yet.

"Don't even think about it."

"What choice do I have, North? This is the reality of being in high school. Unlike my brilliant brother, I haven't been accepted to college yet. I still need to be a good student or else watch my future go down the drain."

North looked like he wanted to say something, but didn't argue with my point.

I wept silently, wiping tears away and tried to remind myself that in the bigger picture, when I looked back at my life, maybe this situation would be something I would laugh at and grow from. Something that wouldn't be a big deal. Something that would just be a speck because my future bands would be awesome and we would be winners every season...but I knew I was kidding myself. This was a special night, never to be repeated and instead of having a front row seat like I deserved, I wasn't even going to be a spectator. I bitterly knew Ms. Jenkins would have no clue if I snuck in the back and watched, but as my anger took over the sadness I was feeling, I resented even being near the field. More than anything, I wanted to find Jude and make him drive me home.

"What are you thinking?" North asked.

"I should just go."

"Why would you do that?"

"I'm not wanted here."

"You really think that?"

"I don't know what to think. All I want to do is go back in time and not text you. Or, not give my phone to Jude. Or further back to a time when you had never dated her."

"Look, Denise will get hers. You seriously can't put out such bad karma like that and not expect it to come back. At this point, I want to forget she exists. Right now we need to focus on you and getting you to the awards ceremony."

"We need a distraction. We need a genuine emergency to distract Ms. Jenkins. Maybe something could happen to someone in the band…" I had a very specific someone in mind.

"We're not going to hurt anyone, Rigby."

"I wasn't thinking of that," I lied, then asked, "And you think an appeal is out of the option?"

"I didn't get the feeling she knew what to do. I doubt she ever thought she would encounter a situation like ours in her teaching career."

I forced myself to put ourselves in our band director's shoes.

"There you guys are! I was about to activate your GMS – I've been looking for you all day." An out of breath Jude came running up to us and as much as I wanted to blame my brother for his part in all this, I just couldn't do it. The look on his face was enough. Jude asked, "So, what happened?"

I answered, "Ms. Jenkins is choosing to bust us on the text messages."

He looked between me and North and said, "What kind of text messages?"

As comfortable as I was with my twin, I didn't want to go into the details and responded, "Private ones, Jude."

My brother sank down heavily on the bench next to me, "I should've known. This is my fault."

"It's no one's fault but Denise's and I won't hear you say another word about it."

"I thought I knew what I was doing."

"You're used to dealing with high school girls, Jude, not devious college chicks bent on revenge. Seriously, it's not your fault."

"I didn't think she would have an agenda of her own."

"Believe me, no one know better than I do, Denise can be very convincing. I think we should avoid focusing on the punishment and more on a solution. Let Ms.

Jenkins think she 'won' for now, but you need to be out on the field tonight, Rigby."

"What did she decide to do?" Jude asked.

"I have to sit out the finals." I managed to get the words out without choking.

"Well, that's not cool." My brother, master of the understatement.

"Tell me about it."

Jude cracked his knuckles and stood up, "How much time do we have left?"

I looked at my phone, a device I wanted to toss and never see again. For all the good memories I had attached to it, were now tainted by Denise and her inability to see two people happy. The dinner break was now over, and the top ranked, largest bands were going to take the field. Whatever we could hope to come up with, our chances seemed impossible. I answered sadly, "One hour, maybe an hour and a half at the most."

Jude paced back and forth for a few moments, then snapped his fingers dramatically and announced, "I have an idea."

I perked up. My brother was usually reliable, and in this crisis, I would take any suggestion. I said, "Go ahead."

"What was the name of that school who gave you crap earlier in the season?"

"Harrison-Benavidez?"

"Whoever. They're here, right?"

I nodded skeptically, unable to connect how my more or less enemies being here was going to help us accomplish much of anything.

"Look, I wasn't named after the patron saint of lost causes for nothing. Maybe it's time to make friends with them..."

Nearly an hour to an hour and half later, I still couldn't believe what I, well, we, had accomplished. I guess, when people put their minds to something, anything can (and occasionally does) happen. It had taken a bit of luck, and a lot of circumstance, but somehow our plotting had come together. Of all the ways I pictured this day going, this was one of the least likely scenarios. Of course, I never expected my band director to read personal my personal texts either, so maybe this was just the way things were destined to play out.

My new friend, Melanie (the snarky redhead from earlier in the season) looked over at me, as if she also, did not believe the situation either. Given the circumstances, it was too weird to even try and figure out what to say to each other, so we both kept quiet.

The taller guy, and only male drum major, Kevin, instructed me, "Just be sure to stand in the back."

From behind Kevin's uniformed shoulder, I could see my own small band gathering as we all walked across the grass in preparation of the awards ceremony.

Danielle, the other drum major, and the nicest one from the trio (and perhaps, the one most interested in my brother) looked at me and asked, "What will you do if you win?"

"We're not going to win," I replied, then added, "Seriously, it's just enough I get to be out here. I really appreciate what you guys have done for me."

Here, of course, was the field. Here, was also with the Harrison-Benavidez high school marching band leadership. Between Jude's flirting, North's random friendship with some of the other instructors at HB, and my ability to suck it up and apologize, we had somehow talked my way (HB uniform and all) onto the field. The announcer's voice cut off my future comments and thoughts. I looked down the field at the various bands that had lined up, but was only able to glimpse the top of Everett's head.

What if we did win? What would I do then?

The maroon and white uniform felt strange on me, but underneath all the polyester was a loyal Parktown

Pirate. It didn't matter if I was wearing a HB uniform, or was sectioned with their leadership. What mattered was that I was on the field. In this moment, I had no regrets. I had started this season and was going to see it through. I doubted anyone in my band would ever know what I had done to get on the field, and wondered what sort of crazy lie Ms. Jenkins must have come up with to explain my absence. Still, I was proud of my commitment, and also more than a little touched by the actions of my boyfriend and brother. Although I couldn't see them I knew North had rejoined our band and Ms. Jenkins, while Jude had promised to run interference with our still in the dark parents.

While the band traded inside jokes and other random comments around me, I stayed silent. I didn't expect them to be quiet as our scores, tucked away in the Division AA schools category, were announced. We were given Superior ratings, but there was nothing said about our specific numbers. Still, I stood up a little taller, knowing we had at least done that well and not completely embarrassed ourselves on the field today.

It was Everett who walked across the green grass to accept the Superior trophy and I felt a weird stab of jealousy. I knew it was petty and shallow to want to walk across and be recognized in front of everyone, but I did want that. I wanted to stride proudly with my drum majorette boots and whistle and have everyone see I was the one in charge. Still, even tucked behind a bunch of students from a rival school was somehow better than being stuck in some cold bus, sitting with one of the band parents. Here, at least, I could be a witness to my band's success.

The HB crew jumped to attention where it was their turn. Fortunately, they also received Superiors, so I didn't have to worry about any awkwardness. Plus, it was fun to get caught up in their excitement. Even though I hadn't gone to school with these kids, the emotions were the same. We had all put in long hours on practice fields, sweating in the summer, earning our tan lines. We all had stories of losses and wins, parades and missed steps. In spite of ourselves, I shared a nostalgic smile with Danielle.

Then, without warning, the moment of truth arrived. Captions.

I had seen other bands perform throughout the day and knew we wouldn't be taking home anything special. I knew being invited to this event was our big win. So, I enjoyed seeing the other bands squeal and delight at their awards. I wasn't jealous or envious, if anything, I was charged to bring those feelings to my students one day.

So, imagine my surprise when the drum major category came up.

I had been so lost in my own little world, I didn't realize suddenly everyone was staring at me.

The announcer's voice carried over the stadium, "In third place, will the drum major from Parktown High School please come forward and accept the award?"

No one from my school budged. Whether defiance or from shock, no one moved forward.

From the field, where the announcer was standing, I could tell there was some confusion. People in the stands began to whisper among themselves. The Harrison-Benavidez group shifted nervously.

"Last call, will a representative from the Parktown marching band please come forward to pick up their trophy?" The voice carried more than a hint of annoyance in it.

The whispers in the crowd quickly turned into a buzz. This was a major regional invitational and it was completely against protocol not to go up and get one's award.

"What are you waiting for?" Melanie turned around and asked me, "Go up there."

What was I waiting for?

For someone to tell me it was okay? To get permission for something I had earned?

I pushed through the Harrison-Benavidez group and stepped forward.

The crowd instantly hushed.

With one foot in front of the other, I continued walking perfect 8 to 5 steps.

As I was strutted proudly across the field, I saw Ms. Jenkins staring at me. I looked defiantly in her direction and continued my march. I saw Denise next to her and changed my look from proud grin to disrespectful smirk. I was moving on to bigger things than this stadium and the small program I had turned around. I had North and a third place drum major trophy waiting for me. Speaking of my favorite instructor, I found him and my smirk turned into a genuine smile. He had been worth it – the waiting, the build up, the stress – all of it had led us to today and I knew after all we had been through, we had earned the future ahead.

Finally, I looked back at my Parktown crew. Everett flashed me a thumbs up, while the rest of the gang did a weird combination clapping, saluting, laughing thing. I found myself unexpectedly getting choked up.

By the time I got to the judges, I think they realized I was not from the Parktown section of the crowd, but what were they going to do?

I gave them a big smile and, accepting my small piece of plastic, said politely, "Sorry for the wait, sometimes I like to make an entrance."

In the end, we placed 20th out of 27 bands competing. No one seemed to care very much. In fact, after the awards ceremony when we had reconvened with the rest of the band, they were all excited about why I was still (inexplicably) wearing a Harrison-Benavidez uniform. In the moment, lying to my band was more difficult than I imagined it would be and I was glad when Jude came to my rescue. Putting a hand on my shoulder, my brother said, "Imagine it – I had just gone to the food stand and got a heaping pile of nachos..."

I watched everyone's eyes get wide – nachos, while delicious, were a fearful adversary of any marching band member's uniform.

Sensing my cue to jump in, I interrupted, "I had just changed back into my drum major uniform and came up behind him."

"She tapped me on the shoulder—"

"Scaring him completely!"

Jude shot me a dirty look, but said, "And she accidently ended up with all of the nachos down the front of her uniform."

We had the crowd on edge now, and if we could just bring our fake story home, no one ever had to know about me, North and Ms. Jenkins. I continued, "I ran to the busses, but they were all locked and I couldn't find a driver anywhere."

"I was with her and, even though I knew about the backstory with HB, understood there was no time to mess around." Popping his collar suavely, he continued with a basic version of what had actually happened, "I had a chat with a few of the members and secured my lovely sister a uniform."

Everett had joined the group and asked, "Then why didn't you join us on the field? We were looking for you everywhere."

North had managed to find us and added his part, "The Harrison-Benavidez director was already suspicious. I had to distract him. We had to make a last minute decision."

As a final comment to sway everyone, I pleaded, "I had to get on the field."

Whether or not anyone suspected the real drama which had taken place, Everett was nice enough to say, "Well, however you managed it – congratulations."

"Thank you. Now, I think I need to return my uniform – I'll meet everyone at the busses."

North joined me and I asked, "Have you talked to Denise yet?"

"Yes. I don't think she'll be bothering us anytime soon."

"What did you tell her?" Part of me was a bit upset I wouldn't get my face off with his ex-girlfriend and the young woman who had come so close to destroying my perfect season.

"Things I should have told her a long time ago. I realize I didn't do you, me, or anyone else any favors by not confronting her a long time ago. I should have pulled her aside the first day she showed up at Parktown. I should have told Nancy I didn't want her here. Instead, I did nothing."

"You can't blame yourself."

"I do. If nothing else this season, I feel like I've grown up a lot."

"And not having references?"

"Not that big a deal."

"Really?"

"I never told you why I came to Parktown, did I?"

"No."

"Basically, I saw a posting at the school of music – Ms. Jenkins was looking for help. She didn't have a big budget."

"And?"

"And I went home and looked you guys up."

In response, I cringed and said, "And you still came?"

"You really only had one place to go."

"Up?"

"Exactly. So, while I might not have a recommendation, all I have to do is send a video from last season and one from tonight – my work will speak for itself."

"So, it's 'your' work, is it?"

Looking around, he leaned into me and said, "I might have had some help."

I wished we could hold hands, but didn't want to risk anything further. We walked in silence a moment, when North asked, "Before we were interrupted, what were you going to say earlier?"

"When?"

"When we were standing with your parents. Were you going to tell them about us?"

"No. Actually, I was going to tell all of you – I think I know what I want to major in."

"And that would be?"

"Music education."

"Really?"

"Really. I don't know why it took me so long to come around to it. What do you think?"

He didn't answer right away, and I was a bit scared what he was going to "You know I have to ask. I just want to be clear you're doing this for you and it has nothing to do with me and our relationship."

"I'd be lying if I said it didn't have a little to do with you, but honestly, I've never been happier than this season. Even when things were bad, there is nowhere else I would rather be. The fact I could get paid to be around students... I don't know, it seems kind of fantastic."

"It's not all fun and games, you know."

"Music theory?"

"That and a lot of other things, but have no fear, I have no doubt you'll conquer them like you did becoming a drum major."

"So, you think I can do it?"

"I have no doubt about it."

With that, we approached the Harrison-Benavidez group. Many of them were still in various stays of undress, so I slipped right in, turning to North and indicating my zipper, asked, "Do me?"

"Happy to."

After thanking the drum majors for the use of their uniform and spot on the field, North and I made our way back to where the Parktown buses were parked. North went over to the equipment truck while I mingled with the rest of the band. Jude caught up with me and before he could say anything, I said, "Since I don't think I've said it, thanks for all your help today. There's no way I would've made it through this season without you."

"Give yourself some credit, sis."

"Think you can handle yourself with those college girls next year, bro?" I asked, noticing Denise skulking in the background.

"You're never going to let me live this down, are you?"

"Not for a little while."

"I guess I deserve it."

"Look, even if I won't believe you, can you at least tell me that you'll call one of those drum majors?" One of the big reasons I had been allowed on the field had been Jude's flirtatious promise to 'return the favor' with somehow both of the HB drum majors, and perhaps their feature twirler, if I wasn't mistaken.

"I did promise I would, didn't I?" He gave me a sheepish grin.

"Yeah, yeah, I've heard that before."

"Don't worry about me, sis, I think I might be turning over a new leaf."

"Oh yeah? Why's that?"

"I realized you and North have a cool thing going. It might be time to try monogamy for awhile."

"I'll believe it when I see it."

"What's that?" North asked, joining us from finishing up at the equipment truck.

"Seems Jude might give up his dating ways."

"Well, keep those skills sharp, buddy, it's what got you on the field today."

"See you back at home, sis. Take care of her, North."

"You got it."

Although almost everyone was on the bus, I wasn't surprised to see Ms. Jenkins approach us. North tensed beside me, but she held up her hands and said, "I want to tell you a story."

I nodded and she continued, "Maybe this is too personal, and maybe I shouldn't be telling you, but here goes nothing. Once upon a time I was in college, being a good student, working hard."

"And?"

She scuffed her heeled foot on the ground and said, "And I had a crush on one of my professors."

North and I exchanged contained surprised glances, but didn't say anything.

"And it didn't go anywhere. I knew he knew I liked him. He didn't handle it as well as he could, but for the most part, he spared my feelings. Later I would realize I was way too immature to know what I was dealing with." She gestured to us and said, "So seeing you two, I don't know – something about it brought up emotions I thought I had long put behind me. I know it's not much of an apology and it won't make up for earlier today."

With the buses idling behind us, we were silent, until I asked, "Did it occur to you things might work out for us? That we might be different."

"Rigby, I see so much potential in you. I didn't want anything to happen that would jeopardize your future. Over the semester, you've made me realize so many things about the program – I know you'll make some band very proud one day."

I smiled and answered, "North is my future. Yes, I may be naïve and optimistic, but I really believe in us."

She looked at us a long moment and said, "I hope he is."

With that comment, she moved to get on the bus, leaving us alone.

"You are."

"I am?"

"Rigby Sullivan, you are one of the most amazing people I've ever met. I can't wait to have you in my future."

So, my senior season came to an unexpected end. I wasn't too sad, because I knew there were still many seasons ahead of me – each with their own stories to tell. This evening was a great start something much bigger. Back at Parktown, slipping my arms tightly around North's waist, we zoomed off into the cold November night. Yes, there were still challenges ahead, but after the season we'd shared together, I thought we were capable of facing almost anything.

Fin.

Somewhere over Europe (en route to London), July 17, 2009

Doha, Qatar, final draft, October 5, 2012

Afterword

When I sat down to write The Line in 2005, I had no idea what I was doing – where it would lead me, who I would meet. I didn't have a clue that my journey would lead me to write over 200,000 words about the marching arts, that I would create characters I would become so fond of. And now, seven years later, I'm sitting down revising a final draft of my last marching novel. This is a bittersweet moment. I'm in my office – a place where many an hour has been spent writing new scenes, looking at cover art and interacting with you, the reader. The Line series, along with my stand alone novels, Confessions of a Teenage Band Geek, and the one you just finished reading, Major Pain, have been a true labor of love made possible by motivation from you, the reader.

If you've been with me since the beginning, thank you. For all that you've offered me, I can only give words and scenes and dialogue and hope you've been entertained.

So, what happens next?

Where is a marching author to go?

For the time being, I'll continue to run my marching arts tumblr. I'll also be eagerly awaiting the day when one of my books gets adapted to film or television. In the event that Hollywood does not decide to do this, I plan on checking in every once in awhile – updating the previous books and continuing to support the marching arts how I can.

Until then, my focus will now shift towards three more mature novels I've been working on over the past few years. While I still have an unpublished YA novel, it's out of the realm of marching and I'm not entirely sure what its fate will be yet.

Until then, as ever,
Keep marching.

Courtney

###

ABOUT THE AUTHOR
AND HER BOOKS

Ms. Brandt is proud to present The Line, and the additional novels in the complete series, A Fine Line, Keeping in Line, and The Line Up. Each of the lighthearted novels was created for high school students and alumni in marching band. As a former drumline member, Courtney enjoys bringing a fictional voice to band geeks all over the world! Additionally, Courtney was proud to announce the release of Confessions of A Teenage Band Geek in Fall 2011 and her final YA marching novel, Major Pain, in the fall of 2012.

If you enjoy marching band, feel free to follow her Tumblr account dedicated to the marching arts:

http://marchingartsphotos.tumblr.com/

45768452R10115

Made in the USA
Middletown, DE
20 May 2019